Wives and Girlfriends

A novel

Wives and Girlfriends

A novel

By

Nishawnda Ellis

URBAN BOOKS
www.urbanbooks.net

Urban Books
10 Brennan Place
Deer Park, NY 11729

ISBN-13: 978-1-60162-000-2
ISBN-10: 1-60162-000-4

First Printing May 2007
Printed in the United States of America

10 9 8 7 6 5 4 3 2 1

Submit Wholesale Orders to:
Kensington Publishing Corp.
C/O Penguin Group (USA) Inc.
Attention: Order Processing
405 Murray Hill Parkway
East Rutherford, NJ 07073-2316
Phone: 1-800-526-0275
Fax: 1-800-227-9604

Acknowledgments

You never know how truly blessed you are until you look around and realize the gift of life.

I would like to thank all my supporters who made my dream of becoming a published author a reality. I promise to continue to give you nonstop, drop-dead drama that, at one time or another, reflects a little of all of us.

Mom, Dad, Grandma, Tiffanie, Charles JR, Charnai, Adrian, Kamari, Jayden, George, Uncle Snook, Naday, Jayme, Nanci, Damian, Ms. Gerri, and the Reid and Ellis families, I love you all so much and am so proud to be a part of the family.

To my friends, Krishona, Yaneke, Andrea, Kizzy, Judith, Jamila, Ayana, Christina, Zakiya, Adam, Charles, Jennifer, Gregory, Dwayne, Jennifer B, Kenyetta, Kesawn, Selene, Roscoe, Silkeya, Boog, my MGH family, and Duane, your energy keeps me so motivated, and I will never forget any of you.

To Ebony Expressions Book Club and Reading Divas Book Club, thank you so much for supporting my first novel.

To Lloyd from the Black Library, thanks for promoting my book signing and your continued support for the Boston Book Bazaar.

To Karibu Books and all the other bookstores that have shown their support, thank you.

To SORMAG, for their continued support of Black authors and featuring me in their June/July issue, thank you.

Acknowledgments

To all the authors I've met on the road, in writing groups, AHA, BWUnited, New England Black Writers and who supported the Boston Book Bazaar, thank you for taking a chance on a first-time event. Last year was fun; this year will be even better.

To all the supporters of the Boston Book Bazaar's first year, may you continue to support this wonderful event. Thank you so much.

And last but definitely not least, thank you, too, all the readers who supported my debut novel and wrote great reviews and continue to e-mail me with comments and enthusiasm for my work. Continue to support Black Authors, especially self-published and small Publishers. We're on the rise.

Hugs and Kisses.

Nish

CAUGHT UP

"Daddeeeee, telephone!"

Dominic paused for a moment. *Who could be calling at this hour?* "I got it, Dawson. Hang up."

A female vixen's voice came through the earpiece. "I need to see you."

Once Dominic recognized the voice, he whispered, "You know damn well that isn't possible! How the hell did you get this number?"

"I'll tell you when I see you. Meet me at our spot in one hour."

"An hour? Now I know you have lost your mind, Tera. You will be waiting forever because I'm not seeing you tonight."

"You sure are, Mr. 'Dick-me-down' Jones.'"

"Look, I told you I can't. We're in the middle of dinner."

"I don't really care. One hour, Dominic."

Donna yelled from the living room, "Dominic, we are having dinner. Who are you talking to?"

* * *

Dominic raced back home before Donna realized it was after one a.m. He couldn't believe how the tables had turned against him. He used to get so much pleasure from being able to sleep with Tera then going home to play his role as the perfect husband. It had never dawned on him that his unfaithful ways would finally catch up to him, that one day, he would lose control and suffer the consequences. He tried to break it off with Tera, but she wouldn't let go, wouldn't accept it. *Guess the loving I gave was too good,* he thought. *I didn't want things to come to this, but what else was I supposed to do?*

Under no circumstances was he willing to leave his family for any woman. He'd considered telling Donna, but that would've just added fuel to the already ignited flame. So Dominic was left with the only solution to his problem—Tera had to go.

Chapter 1

Sunday afternoon was breezy and sunny with a temperature of 72 degrees. The summer heat had disappeared, and fall was going to arrive in two days. Police sirens, an ambulance, and a coroner van parked outside the sixty-nine-apartment Brookline Side Condominiums interrupted the quiet evening. Nosy and concerned neighbors flocked outside their condos to find out what brought the Brookline police to their homes. They soon would discover that it was murder.

"Check the caller ID and last calls the victim made from here," Detective Mark Anderton said. "I want to know who she last spoke to." This was his first murder case since he was promoted to lead detective.

After examining the crime scene, Mark's investigative mind began to go to work. He recorded his comments using a taping device. "African-American woman, age range 21-28, about five feet, seven inches, 135 pounds, found with a gunshot wound to her frontal lobe. Bullet appears to be from a .38 caliber or similar. No signs of forced entry or burglary. However, there are signs of a struggle. Shattered particles of glass cover the living room floor, and the coffee table has been knocked over. Victim appears to have fought the assailant off. Rule out suicide. Does not appear victim shot herself, due to extent of the injury. Also, victim struck with some type of blunt object to the back of the head. However, probable cause of death was a gunshot wound.

"Victim was wearing a pink negligee. Candles appear recently lit and CD player's power still is on. A bottle of champagne, whipped cream and chocolate-covered strawberries were found in the victim's refrigerator, indicating possibly that the victim was expecting company. Her guest may or may not have arrived. The victim was found lying supine on her living room, no weapon or weapons discovered. Not sure of the time of death at this time. A neighbor called the police after hearing a gunshot around 2:15 a.m., making the approximate time of death between 2:00 and 2:10 a.m., according to the condition of the body and the time of neighbor's phone call. Scene indicates victim either knew the assailant or was caught off guard.

"Hey, Johnson, did you get the last incoming and outgoing calls yet? Also, do we have a name and next of kin for the victim yet?"

Officer Johnson shouted from the bedroom, "We're working on identifying the listed names for the last outgoing calls. The victim's name is Tera Larou. No next of kin as of yet. You should come take a look at this. We found the victim's electronic address book, and I must say, she is quite the busy girl—I mean, *was*."

"Johnson, don't disrespect the dead. Bring me the address book and leave your comments at home." Detective Anderton had little tolerance for his co-worker's theatrics.

Officer Johnson entered the living room. "See for yourself. She doesn't have names listed with the phone numbers. Instead they are listed as suitors."

"How many suitors are there?"

"Two hundred and fifty-four."

"Two hundred and fifty-four? Are you kidding me? No names?"

"Nope. Just suitors one through two hundred and fifty-four."

"How the hell can she keep the names straight? Maybe Ms. Larou didn't want anyone to know who she was seeing." *Such a beautiful woman, too. What were you into? Two hundred and fifty-four? I don't think I have been with fifty-four women, let alone two hundred and fifty-four.*

"All right, Johnson, get me the names from the phone numbers of all two hundred and fifty-four, especially the last five. And find out if she owns this condo, where she works, if she pays her own bills, the name her car is in. I want to know everything about this woman. Do we have the names for those calls yet?" Detective Anderton was growing inpatient.

"I'll check with Riley." Johnson disappeared back into Tera's bedroom.

Detective Anderton was left alone with his thoughts. *What could she have done to these men to make someone want her dead?*

Officer Johnson returned with Mark's requested information. "The last incoming call was from a woman named Shaniece Turner, and the last outgoing call was made to Dominic Jones.

"Check the last outgoing call number to see if it matches any of the numbers in her address book."

"Already ahead of you. It doesn't, but the last suitor's number is a cell phone number, 617-555-8211, and guess what?"

"Johnson."

"Lighten up. I just had Riley check it, and the number belongs to Jones IT Consultants."

Detective Anderton looked confused.

"You don't know who Dominic Jones is, do you?"

"Should I?"

"You should. He's one of the wealthiest black men in this city, Dominic Jones of Jones IT Consultants."

"I don't care if he is the wealthiest man in the world. He's a suspect, as well as all those other two hundred and fifty-three suitors in Ms. Larou's book. Get me an address for Mr. Jones. I have a few questions for him."

"I think you better check with the chief first."

"Why?"

"Because not only is Mr. Jones wealthy, he sponsors Mayor Menning's campaigns. The guy is loaded and, from what I understand, protected. You get what I'm saying? Almost untouchable."

"I guess I am about to reach out and touch Mr. Untouchable. I have a murder case to solve. Nothing or no one is more important than that."

"I hear you, but be careful and extra clean on this one. The man is not to be messed with."

Detective Anderton smirked. "Apparently, he's got you under his wing. Save it, Johnson. Get me the address."

"Fine. You're the lead detective. You know what you're doing."

"That I am, Johnson, and that I do."

Chapter 2

Six Months Earlier

Dominic Jones wiped the steam-fogged bathroom mirror and smiled. He examined his body obsessively. He made an Incredible Hulk pose four times and spun around, admiring his six-pack abdomen, toned pectorals, burly biceps and triceps, tight gluteus maximus, and muscular calves. Each time he turned, he smiled at himself in the mirror and grunted through his frosty white teeth. He ran his fingers through his curly black hair and began to apply his shaving cream. He winked at himself each time he stroked the razor downward. He splashed his face with water, dried with a fresh towel, and then put on a dash of aftershave. He brushed his teeth, flossed, and gargled with Listerine. He smiled and winked at himself one more time. He recited to himself, "I see pride. I see power. I see one bad muthafucka who don't take shit from no one."

Dominic retired to his master bedroom, where his wife

Donna was lathering her body with her Avon products at her vanity table. He kissed her cheek. "My, my, don't we taste like candy. Be careful, I might want a sweet snack before we go."

Donna spun around her sitting stool and ripped off his bath towel, leaving him buck-naked. "I might just want a snack of my own." She proceeded to take Dominic into her mouth as she stroked his penis with her tongue and lips, no teeth. Donna performed oral sex on her husband at the drop of a hat. She would do anything to please him and keep him happy. As she bobbed her head back and forth, she let out a sensual moan.

Dominic's eyes rolled to the back of his head, as his other head was being caressed in the way only his loving wife could. He never got in the way of Donna's eagerness to please him. He not only encouraged it, he expected it at least twice a day. It wasn't a secret as to who was in charge. Dominic liked things in order, and at that moment, Donna was falling in line.

As Donna sucked harder and longer on Dominic's shaft, he felt himself begin to tremble. Donna knew that signal all too well as she prepared to swallow her husband's seeds of life. When he ejaculated, she didn't let any of his sperm go to waste.

He handed her a tissue from her nightstand to wipe her lips and face. To his surprise, Donna didn't have any holes in her mouth. She'd knocked back all of his juices.

He kissed her lightly on the lips. "We have to be ready in half an hour."

Donna got dressed within the specified time and was ready to accompany her husband to the United Negro College Fund benefit dinner. Although she'd helped organize the event, her husband was the contributing sponsor and speaker. Donna always loved for her husband to shine, so she arranged a stretch limousine to transport them, and bought herself a corsage to go with her $8,000 black evening gown. She preferred wearing black because, in the past fifteen years, she had gone from a size seven to a size fourteen. She still had beautiful, smooth, brown skin, dark brown water chestnut-shaped eyes, and voluptuous lips. She looked healthy as well as gorgeous, standing at five-foot, five and 180 pounds.

Dominic never pressured her to lose weight and seemed as attracted to her as when they'd first met. All the same, Donna prided herself on being the best dressed, most respected, and classiest wife everywhere they went, and adapted to her new look by wearing clothes that complemented her figure and made her feel less self-conscious about being overweight.

Donna took great pleasure in coordinating everything for the dinner, from the table arrangements to the program. She enjoyed being Dominic's right hand, secretary, personal assistant and cheerleader. During their fifteen years of their marriage, she supported her husband mentally, physically, and spiritually. Dominic was her soul mate and she would never disappoint him willingly.

Except for that one thing, she thought. Before sadness entered her heart, she pushed those insecure and guilty feelings out of her head and began to pray. "Lord, please don't let anything go wrong tonight. You are my Lord and Savior, and I put this night, as I have so many other nights, in Your hands. You owe me that, at least. Amen."

Donna broke out in a sweat when she couldn't find her

platinum four-carat diamond studs. *The limo will be here in two minutes.*

Dominic re-appeared in their bedroom with a small black velvet box behind his back.

Donna sensed his presence and began to perspire a little more. She knew he would flip out if she caused him to be late for his benefit dinner. She froze, a look of worry on her face.

He smiled and gave her the black velvet box.

"What is this?" she asked.

"Open it."

To Donna's surprise, he had bought her a pair of 8 ct. diamond earrings mounted in platinum. Donna hugged him with sheer joy and French-kissed him.

Dominic pushed her away and smiled. "Let's not get carried away. We have a dinner to attend. We can finish where we left off afterwards." He playfully smacked her behind. "Put the earrings on and let's go."

"Thank you for the gift, sweetheart. Where are my other platinum studs?"

"I turned them in and upgraded to those," he said, lying through his teeth. "You like them better, right?"

"I love them."

"I thought you would. You deserve the best."

Donna smiled and wiped her perspiration away with a tissue. She was in la-la land, as Dominic led her by the hand down the steps.

They stopped and said good night to their daughter, Dawson, who was playing a video game and talking on the phone to one of her girlfriends. She was a typical spoiled teenager, whose parents pressured her to get excellent grades, attend a prestigious college, and stay a virgin until she got married. All her life she had attended private school and had no problem competing with the brightest kids in her school. She was popular, beautiful, and rich. What else could a fifteen-year-old desire? According to Dawson, her life was perfect. And so was her father.

Donna kissed her only child on the forehead. "Good night, baby. Don't stay up too late and don't leave the house or open the windows. I'm putting the alarm on before we leave."

Dominic looked at his watch. "Donna, we are going to be late. Stop nagging the girl." He turned to his daughter. "Good night, baby."

Dawson paused the game and told her girlfriend to hold on. She ran and hugged her father. "I love you, Daddy."

"I love you, too. See you later."

Confident and in control of his family, Dominic led Donna out by the hand. And so the Joneses left their mansion and proceeded to their benefit dinner, ready to have a remarkable evening.

Chapter 3

Tera began to get ready for the United Negro College Fund benefit dinner. She picked out a black satin halter dress that was cut low and deep in the front, catering to her size 36-D twins, and which stopped right above the knees. Any higher and her cleavage wasn't going to be the only part of her body on display. A matching set of Beyoncé Knowles-style silver dangling earrings and silver necklace hanging between her taped up breasts completed her outfit. She was pushed up and ready to push out on the town in search of her next suitor. Tera pulled out all the stops and never made any apologies for the way she carried herself. The way she saw it, this was her world and she controlled everyone in it.

"Shaniece, hand me those silver rhinestone sandals," Tera demanded.

"I thought you said I could wear them tonight," Shaniece whined, something she always did when she knew Tera was going to have her way.

"I changed my mind. My outfit is calling for them. Just like any man I come close to." Tera laughed as she stared herself down in the mirror. "Damn! If beauty was a crime, I'd be serving a life sentence." She flashed a devilish grin in the mirror.

"What am I suppose to wear with my shimmy dress then?"

"Don't know, don't care. Find something, 'cause I am wearing those shoes."

"I thought you said tonight was about me."

"It is, but in order for me to show you the ropes, I have to dress the part. Tonight is watch and learn. Then you can show and tell, sweetie. Take it from me, an outfit is not complete unless you have all the right equipment." Tera took another glance in the mirror. "And, honey, this body and this face has to have an outfit that complements it. Pure elegance matched with sexiness. So those shoes, the dress, and this body are a total package. Understand?"

Shaniece shook her head. She hated it when Tera was right and hated it even more when Tera turned everything around. "Well, I'm just not going then."

"Fine. But you will never learn how to have James eating out of the palm of your hand. You see the way I make men drool over me. If you want that, you have to watch and learn. First, you bait him, then you play him, and then you act like you worship him. Just when he thinks he has you, you flip the switch on him again, so he doesn't even know what day of the week it is. All he knows is you and all he cares about is when is the next time he gets to be with you."

"Then you get married and live happily ever after, right?"

Tera looked at Shaniece as if she were a dodo bird. "NO!

Have you been paying attention to anything I said? Listen to me, Shaniece, and listen good. If you want all you can get out of a man, know that marriage ain't it. Trust me, it pays not to be the one waiting at home with the kids, wondering where in the hell your husband is at this time of night."

"Then what am I doing this for? I want James to marry me and leave his wife."

"Why? So he can turn around and do the same thing to you?"

"It wouldn't happen that way, Tera. It just wouldn't."

"Oh, would you get your head out of the clouds, Shaniece! Answer me this, did James tell you he was married when you met him?"

"No."

"When you found out, did he say he was leaving her for you?"

"Not in so many words, but I could feel he wanted to."

"What you were feeling was his hard-on, which was about to need ice. Once James knew you knew he was married, he knew it was back to porno and hand lotion because his selfish, stingy wife still thinks she can control a man with sex. Whatever you felt or whatever he told you was to keep him from going back to that. Bottom line."

"No. He was implying that what we had worked for him and that some day we would be together exclusively."

"What he was implying is that you two could continue having an affair, as long as you were down with it."

"I was at first, but I started to get jealous and hated the fact that she got all his time and attention."

"Shaniece, who needs time and attention, when you get

15

designer clothes and expensive cars from him? She is his priority. She is his wife, and you are his girlfriend—Learn the fucking rules."

"But, I don't want to be his girlfriend. I want to be his wife."

"Again, why? Trust me, you are better off being the girl-friend. The benefits are endless. Stick with me and I will show you a world where the girlfriend is what little girls should be dreaming about. Not white picket fences, a dog, and two kids. They should be dreaming about penthouses, exotic getaways, expensive jewelry, and a maid to clean up after your mess, instead of you cleaning up after a husband, children, and a fucking shitty-ass dog. Being a girlfriend has its advantages. It's the only way to be satisfied with men completely, because you are satisfied with yourself and the situation."

"But I love James. I don't want material things, I want him all to myself."

"Why? He doesn't want you all to himself. Shaniece, you must learn to share. As long as your piece is the most ex-pensive, who cares? I could give a shit about love."

"I do, Tera. That's why I can't do this."

"Well, keep singing your sad love songs if you want. I know where that leads . . . to the road of broke, pregnant, and aban-doned. Trust me, that isn't a road any woman should have to travel."

"Well, if that is where it leads me, then fine. I can't be like you."

"Of course not. Because if you could, we wouldn't be hav-ing this conversation. Obviously, love hasn't taken you to the place it has taken me. Best believe, one day it will, and when it does, I will be more than happy to show you why it pays to be a girlfriend rather than a wife. Face it, some women are meant to be girlfriends, and some are meant to be wives." Tera left her cousin with that thought and went to check the messages on her phone.

Tera stayed here and there with family until she finally found a home with her maternal grandmother and Shaniece. Although the two cousins were about the same age, Tera's grandmother treated her like the black sheep of the family. In fact, from the day she was born, her grandmother resented her because her mother had had her at fifteen, her grandmother always looking at her as her daughter's biggest mistake. Tera's mother ended up running off and marrying her father, who was ten years older than she.

One day her parents left her in their car at the mall and were never heard from again. After that, Tera was moved from foster home to foster home then to family members, until her grandmother finally decided to take her in. Tera couldn't stand her grandmother and hated always having to take the blame for everything her mother did. (She'd learned that both of her parents were hooked on drugs.) When Tera turned eighteen, she moved out of her grandmother's home and had been on her own ever since.

Every night she would cry herself to sleep, wishing her father could have loved her like he'd promised and that her mother could have been there for her like she'd promised. She could never figure out why her parents left her. She'd blamed it all on them getting married so young and vowed never to get married or let a man ruin her life the way her grandmother claimed her father did.

Deep down Tera knew where Shaniece was coming from,

but her own experiences with men made her choose and believe in her own way. It was like a religion or craft that she had adopted. Why belong to "The First Wives Club," when being a girlfriend has so much more to offer minus the emotional baggage? Tera was happy with herself and her beliefs, which taught her to never get emotionally attached to her suitors. Once they started to become attached, her idea was to get everything and find a new suitor. Her religion paid her bills, bought her cars, jewelry, vacations, and anything she wanted. It bought her this condo in Brookline and set aside a nice sizable bank account that allowed her to go shopping, and have manicures, pedicures, and her hair done every week. Tera would be damned if she ever went back to thinking like Shaniece. Being a girlfriend was way too much fun and kept her from having to work a nine-to-five bullshit job.

Tera picked up her phone to check her voicemail.

The automatic voice began, *You have two new messages. To hear your messages, press one. First message, Saturday six-thirty p.m.—"Tera, it's Jacob. After giving it much thought, I don't think I'm going to be able to do what we discussed. Call me later."*

Next message, Saturday eight p.m.—"Tera, it's Jacob again. I really need to see you so we can talk. Call me after eleven p.m. I will be available then, or you can just leave me a message. Talk to you soon."

You have no more messages.

Tera ended her call with a huge grin. One of the reasons for attending this benefit dinner was to show Shaniece how she operated. The second was to find a new suitor and get

18

rid of Jacob—after he gave her one hundred thousand dollars.

Showing up at her condo unannounced, demanding she drop what she was doing, or who, for that matter, and tend to his needs, Jacob had worn out his welcome in Tera's book and was fast becoming a liability. She knew the moment she refused, he would cut her off. She couldn't allow him to behave that way or cut out on her without some sort of compensation, so before he got rid of her, she had to get rid of him. But first, there'd be a price to pay, indeed.

Chapter 4

"As I stand here tonight looking at all of my beautiful black people, I know that Martin Luther King, Jr. wasn't the only one who had a dream. The United Negro College Fund has a dream. To see the faces of its youth on the cover of *Forbes* and *Essence* magazines, leading this country as the first African-American president, piloting the first spacecraft to settle on Mars, and finding a cure for the AIDS virus. This organization has a dream to further our youth and teach them to rise above our differences for a brighter future for all, a dream so obscure, only our people can see.

"Help me today, my people, to see that these children, standing on our shoulders and needing us to lift them now, are our future, that they have opportunities and privileges that were not an option for us. Our future depends on these children to lead the next generation and to take care of us when we no longer can take care of ourselves. I implore you to dig deep down in your pockets and give all you can to keep this dream alive. Thank You." Dominic sipped his Perrier as the audience clapped and cheered his speech. He was king and these were his followers. He was on top, and no one could tell him any different. He watched Donna in all her glory as she led the crowd in a standing ovation.

Dominic waved his arms and started to do "the Bankhead bounce" to the music of the jazz band that started playing at the end of his speech. Victory was in the air.

For the rest of the evening Donna charmed every wealthy couple in the room in an effort to raise money for the cause she had helped put together. Capitalizing on her husband's powers of persuasion, she sashayed around and played her part as Mrs. Dominic Jones.

Meanwhile, like a wolf in sheep's clothing, Dominic was doing some cruising of his own. After meeting and greeting the heavyweights of the city, he found his mind wandering to the black thighs, behinds, and faces he came across. As Dominic continued his scavenger hunt, he ran into Jacob Evans. Dominic smiled as his sworn "frienemy" shook his hand. Although both his wife and Jacob's adored each other since college, these men played cordial but secretly despised each other.

For years Dominic and Jacob fought over the limelight in Boston. At the time Dominic's company was getting off the ground, Jacob held the title of richest black man in Boston. In earlier days, Jacob's gained part of his fortune working as a stockbroker on Wall Street in New York.

After realizing his entrepreneurial potential, he started a development company, contracting the city of New York's Housing Authority as his first client. His company, Evans

Steele, named after his father (Evans) and his mother's maiden name (Steele), made millions in the first year and a half building affordable homes in communities in New Rochelle and Mt. Vernon, as well as restoring brownstones in Manhattan.

Unfortunately, his mother fell sick to cancer, and he had to return to Boston. Jacob soon realized the market was wide open for his development company, so he tapped into it and soon built the only minority-owned hotel and suites in the city of Boston.

Just when the Trailblazers Association nominated him entrepreneur of the year, Dominic Jones's Jones IT Consultants was crowned with the title.

Jacob never thought Dominic Jones would amount to anything and hated him ever since that night. He envied Dominic and wished to God that he had what Dominic had. Every chance he got, he tried to discredit Dominic publicly by bringing up his father's drug-dealing history, but Dominic still reigned as the wealthiest black man in Boston, with the mayor in his pocket, literally, and the women beckoning.

"You had to go there with the Martin Luther King speech, didn't you?" Jacob sipped his scotch.

"You know it. I'm sure it will get the response I knew it would, and folks will donate large amounts of money," Dominic told him.

"You sure got your wife working her magic for you. I doubt Tricia could pull that off. You know how bourgeois she can be. Begging is just not her thing. But your wife seems to have it down pat."

Dominic sipped his glass of spring water. "Speaking of begging, I heard Evans Steele is going after that housing project over on Harvard Street. I could put in a word for you with the mayor."

"That won't be necessary. From what I understand, it's confirmed. Evans Steele *will* be building those low-income, affordable housing units in the summer."

"Really? I thought Daniels and Sons was going after that project. You sure your company will be handling it?"

Jacob decided to change the subject. "How is your daughter doing? She and my son go to the same high school."

"How about that? She's doing fine. All A's, debate team, cheerleading, track team, runs the sophomore choir. She's thinking about studying abroad in England her junior year."

"Wow! That's great. J.R. is busy with his studies. He's thinking about applying to Harvard to study business. He'll run my company some day, keep it in the family, you know."

Dominic's attention drifted to the finest black thighs he'd seen all night. "I'm sorry, Jake, what were you saying?"

"Jacob," he said, correcting Dominic's deliberate nicknaming. "I was just saying how proud I am that I have a son to carry on the family name after I'm long gone."

Dominic sensed Jacob was trying to take jabs at him because he didn't have a son, or anyone for that matter, to carry the family name. "Are you going to the Black Businessmen's gala this year? I've been nominated again."

Jacob grimaced. "I'm thinking about it."

"Well, it's in the bag for me, I'm sure. Maybe next year you'll be nominated. I doubt I can win again after this year."

Before Jacob could answer, Dominic added, "Will you excuse me for a minute? Thanks."

Dominic was hot on the trail of the sexy caramel-chocolate goddess who'd just passed him by in a revealing black cocktail dress.

Jacob, too, noticed the exotic woman walking by. She was all too familiar to him.

She smiled at Dominic and sipped from her wine glass.

Dominic followed each sip of her lips down to her revealing cleavage, tiny waist, and voluptuous hips. *Black thighs, behinds and faces.* He couldn't wait to put his cherry bomb mack down.

Tera gave Dominic an instant "Hey" eye stare before turning around and walking toward the terrace.

Dominic began to follow her.

"Hey, honey," Donna said, interrupting his stride, "your speech was brilliant. Why didn't you tell me you had this 'I have a dream' speech? People loved it so much that I have already raised $425,000 in scholarship money."

Dominic continued to smile and tune Donna out, as he watched this gorgeous vixen turn heads.

Obviously, Jacob Evans wasn't immune because he followed her out to the terrace. He grabbed Tera by the arm. "What the hell are you doing here?"

She snatched away from his grip. "Hi, baby. Don't you look handsome tonight." Before Jacob could respond, she kissed him.

He pulled away immediately. "Are you crazy? My wife is in the next room."

Tera giggled. "Please, Jacob, when have you ever been worried about your wife? You know what I would like? For you to fuck me like you did when we were in Tahiti, buck-naked on the beach." She rolled her eyes back as she reminisced and let out a sensual grunt.

Jacob's manhood began to rise at the thought. "Tera, baby, this is not the time nor the place for this. I said I was going to call you later. We need to talk."

"Talk about what? When have we ever talked?" She grabbed the bulge between his legs and caressed it. Then she whispered in his ear, "I could suck the taste out of you right now."

Jacob almost caved at his inner desires. He removed her hand and grabbed her face as he tongued her down. "You are making me crazy right now. I could fuck the shit out of you, you know that?"

Tera tongued him back then stopped. "Why don't you, then?"

"Later. I will talk to you later."

"Please . . . I don't have later. I want you now. Besides, I might be busy later."

"Busy with what?"

She twirled her hair. "Who knows?"

"I told you before, I don't want you seeing anyone else. I mean it."

Tera smirked. "Well, then fuck me now. I can't keep waiting for you."

"I will meet up with you later. Come on, baby."

"What about the one hundred thousand you promised me? Am I supposed to wait for that too?"

Jacob fixed his tie. "Tera, I told you, I will get you anything you want. I just can't get a hold of the money right now. It's tied up in this new project I am doing. Plus, I told you, I can lease a place for your hair and nail spa. You don't need to buy the space."

"Why do I feel you are not being honest with me?"

"Baby, we can talk about this later. I'll get you anything you need. Just be patient."

Tera had no plans to open a salon. It was just one of her many lies to get money out of her suitors. In the past couple of years, she supposedly was opening a daycare, restaurant, boutique, shelter for abused women, and a bridal shop. She also knew Jacob would give her anything, but a check signed to her. He wanted to continue seeing her on the side, yet dictate to her. She couldn't have that. The sure way to get rid of him was to empty his pockets and make him want her out of his life.

"Jacob, I have been looking all over for you," Tricia said.

Jacob's heart dropped and he began to clam up. "Hey, baby. How's your evening going?"

"Fine. Who's this?"

Before Jacob could say anything, Tera answered, "My name is Melissa Clark from Morgan State University. I am here on behalf of their scholarship fund. Nice to meet you, Mrs. Evans."

"Please call me Patricia."

"Well, Patricia, you have a generous husband here. He has really made my night."

Jacob's heart was racing.

"What do you mean?" Tricia asked.

"Should I explain, Jacob?"

Jacob's palms began to sweat. He couldn't believe what was happening.

Tera took charge once again. "He has promised to donate

one hundred thousand dollars to Morgan State University's business program scholarship, named after its founder, Tera Larou."

"He has? Well, that is wonderful. Jacob, I am so proud of you. Believe me, honey, he has such a tight grip on his wallet, I didn't expect him to donate more than his advice." Tricia giggled. "I keep telling him he has to give back and put that advice where his money is. That's how you'll swim with the rest of the fish, honey." Tricia lovingly patted her husband's hand.

Jacob's nervousness turned to rage. He was on fire.

"I totally agree with you, Patricia. We were just finishing up. So you will be making the check out to the Tera Larou scholarship?"

"Sorry. I don't have my checkbook on me. Like I was saying, I may need to get back to you on that."

"I have the checkbook, honey. I brought it just in case you changed your mind. And I am glad you did. How do you spell that name, Melissa?"

"*T-e-r-a L-a-r-o-u.*"

Tricia wrote the check out as instructed and handed it to Tera. She wished Tera good luck and pulled Jacob off the terrace and back into the reception.

When Tricia wasn't looking, Jacob fixed his pants. He couldn't believe the stunt Tera has just pulled. He swore he would get even with her. *Once a gold digger, always a gold digger.* He chopped the money off as a loss.

Tera was in her glory as she sipped wine glass after wine glass.

The evening was coming to an end, but Dominic's thirst was just beginning. He approached Tera. "Fine as wine."

Tera said, "Excuse me?" with a sexy attitude.

"Did you enjoy your evening?"

"Yes. As a matter of fact, I had a wonderful time."

"Are you from this area?"

"Why? Are you conducting a survey?"

Dominic grinned. "Fair enough. Do you have a name?"

"Depends."

"On?"

"Who's asking?"

"Dominic," Jacob interrupted, "I just might give you a call about that housing project . . . just in case, you know."

Cock-blocker. "Just in case what? I thought you didn't need my help."

"I changed my mind."

Sensing the tension and realizing his opportunity, Jacob introduced Dominic to Tera.

"How do you two know each other?" Dominic asked.

"We go way back. Isn't that right, Tera?"

"Right," she answered, smiling. *THE DOMINIC JONES?*

"Talk to you later, Dominic. Enjoy your night." Jacob walked away thinking, *I just might get my revenge by killing two birds with one stone.*

Dominic said, "Can I call you later, Ms. Larou?"

"Depends."

"This again." Dominic rolled his eyes, but smiled. "On?"

"I see the wedding band, so there is no need to cry on my shoulder later about how unhappy you are and make me promises we both know you can't keep. Why should I give you my telephone number?"

Dominic moved closely to Tera and whispered in her ear, "Because we both know I can give you everything you ever dreamed of. Here is my number. Call me when you're ready for your dreams to start coming true." Dominic left Tera with those thoughts, knowing he would hear from her soon.

Tera was dancing inside. *Mission accomplished.* She had gotten rid of Jacob with a hundred-thousand-dollar bonus and landed the biggest fish in the sea, Dominic Jones. For her, life couldn't be sweeter.

Chapter 5

Dominic held the receiver to his ear and leaned back in his leather office chair. He grinned with delight as Mr. Levy, his accountant, assured him that last week's figures were accurate and Jones IT Consultants was fifteen percent above its quarterly sales quota. *More money, more power, more respect.* "Thanks, Mr. Levy. You've made my day. You should be getting a FedEx package today with two courtside seats for the playoffs tonight."

Mr. Levy loved his Celtics and was waiting patiently for them to be the next NBA champions. He could smell the victory every year, and every year he was disappointed. Nonetheless, he was a devoted fan, and appreciated the incentives that his number-one client gave him. "You didn't have to do that, Dominic, but thank you."

"No problem, man."

"Hey, can I run something by you?"

"Sure."

"I know it's none of my business, but I noticed two months ago a check from your business account was cleared for seventy-five thousand dollars to a Nina Meyers. It was a rather large amount, so I checked your employee files but couldn't get a record of her. I wanted to make sure it wasn't fraud. You know about this?"

"My man always got my financial back. Thanks for looking out, Mr. Levy. That is why I pay you a hefty salary. I authorized that payment. I no longer required Ms. Meyers's services, so I gave her severance pay . . . if you get my drift."

Mr. Levy was silent for a minute, and then he finally caught on. Embarrassed, he said, "Oh, I see. Just making sure you was aware."

"And I appreciate that. Have fun at the game."

"Thanks again, Dominic."

Nina Meyers was Dominic's last girlfriend. They enjoyed long getaways and endless nights of sexing and doting on each other's company. They'd met while Dominic was shopping at Victoria's Secret for a Valentine's Day present for Donna. When the store didn't have the size 38DD Dominic needed for Donna, Nina, the store manager at the time, put an order through and had it to him by the end of the week. Dominic instantly found her attractive and invited her to personally deliver the gift to his office.

Nina thoroughly enjoyed the perks of being Dominic's girl. He would shower her with gifts and at a moment's notice take her to Paris, telling Donna he was on a business trip.

Nina found being his girlfriend to be so time-consuming that she even quit her job to focus on their relationship. Evidently she focused too much, because she was around more than Dominic liked, and their arrangement began to strangle him.

A year into their relationship, he decided to break it off.

A distraught Nina told him she was pregnant.

Dominic gave her his infamous speech about she being the girlfriend, and his intentions never to leave his wife. He offered to pay for the abortion, and Nina pretended to almost go through with it. Until she told him she really wasn't pregnant.

That was the last straw. Dominic cut her off and hoped to never see her again. He first gave Nina Donna's platinum diamond earrings to ease her pain and get her off his back. When she began to really show her ass, following him to business meetings and dinner parties, he paid her off to stay away. That was the last he saw of her.

Dominic longed for someone other than his wife to stroke him and fulfill his desires, so he was back on the market for a woman to fill Nina's shoes. This new meat, Tera, might just prove to be what he was searching for in a playmate. *Only time will tell*, Dominic thought. It'd been like this for so long that he couldn't recall a time when he didn't have a little something extra on the side. It wasn't that he didn't love Donna or his family. He just lusted for the freedom to do whatever he wanted, and that made him happy. However, since he didn't want to hurt Donna, once his girlfriends threatened to jeopardize his family, he cut them off.

After all, Dominic never had a problem finding another girlfriend to take his last girlfriend's place. He didn't mind spending on his women either. He actually enjoyed being able to fill their every need and want. That was exactly what he planned to do with Tera.

His cell phone rang. He didn't recognize the number but answered anyway. "Hello."

"Hello yourself."

"Who is this?"

"Tera Larou. Have you been expecting my call?"

"It's been a week. I thought you forgot about me."

"I've been busy."

"You can tell me all about it over dinner."

"When?"

"Tonight at eight. Give me your address. I'll have a car pick you up."

Tera gave him the requested information and their rendezvous was set.

After hanging up with her, Dominic used his office phone to call Donna. He needed an excuse to skip dinner with her and Dawson.

"Hello," Donna answered.

"Hello, baby. How's your day going?"

"Dawson has a game tonight. The JV cheerleading squad is going to perform during the half-time show. She needs her skirt hemmed and some white shoelaces. I swear that girl waits until the last minute to tell me, so I can go ripping and running. I don't know what her . . ."

Dominic pretended to listen as Donna rambled on and on about their ungrateful, spoiled-rotten daughter. He knew that he'd created a monster by giving his only daughter whatever she wanted, but it just seemed easier to do. He figured, let Donna clean up the messes, he had other things to worry about. After all, he was the breadwinner and provided very well for his family. As long as Dawson excelled in school, behaved and stayed away from horny-ass teenage boys, he was happy.

Donna continued, "I'm thinking we can catch dinner at Maggiano's after the game."

"About dinner . . . I have a meeting that's going to run real late. I have some new clients that might need my help overseas with their IP address for their Internet hosting service."

"Dominic, you know you are speaking French to me."

"Sorry, baby, but I won't be home until late."

"Okay, Dawson will be disappointed you missed probably the only time she will be in a half-time show this year."

"I know. But you can make her understand, right?"

"I always do."

"That's my baby. Don't wait up. I love you."

"I love you too."

Dominic hung up not feeling the least bit guilty. He was too preoccupied with thoughts of the sex escapade he was about to have with his new friend Tera.

Chapter 6

Jacob finished his business meeting with the city councilman, R.J. Jordan. He was furious that his company was passed up for the huge affordable housing project on Harvard Street. Just as Dominic had predicted, Daniels and Sons was hired for the contract. Jacob even suspected that Dominic had something to do with it.

He wanted to release some tension fast, and being on the outs with his girlfriend, finding someone other than his wife to fulfill his needs seemed almost impossible.

Jacob knew Tera was up to something and never believed her when she said she wanted the money for her new business idea. But to beat him out of his money the way she did was distasteful. True, in the long run, giving her one hundred thousand dollars would be much cheaper than going through a divorce if his wife ever found out about his unfaithful ways.

Jacob enjoyed Tera more than she knew, and was very

happy whenever they were together. In all honesty, he missed her. True, he got very jealous whenever he thought she was with other men, but he believed he had the right to demand her full attention. After all, for seven months he was footing her bills, taking her on romantic getaways that he never took his wife to, buying her just about anything she asked for. Part of him loved Tera and the joy she brought to his life. But for her to do what she did was unforgivable.

His feelings were divided. On the one hand he wished he could call her up and make their usual arrangements, but on the other, he wanted to wring her neck and make her suffer for her treachery.

A thought popped in Jacob's mind. *Maybe I really can get even with both my enemies if I play my cards right.* Jacob remembered introducing Tera to Dominic at the benefit dinner. He hoped the seed he'd planted would begin to grow and soon Dominic would suffer Tera. And Tera would finally bite off more than she could chew when dealing with the son of a cold-blooded murderer.

Jacob smiled as he dialed Tera's number, to see if his flower of deceit had started to sprout.

"Hello, Jacob. How are you?" Tera's vanity didn't allow her to avoid Jacob's calls. She had him beaten and wasn't afraid to deal with the fallout.

"How do you think I am? If I wasn't a God-fearing man, I don't think you would be able to answer a phone ever again, bitch."

Tera giggled. "If you were a God-fearing man, you would never have left yourself wide-open like that. Face it, Jacob—You were becoming a liability in this relationship. I just did what any woman would have. I took my compensation for my contribution to making you happy. Trust me, you got off easy. I saved you from alimony."

"And what makes you think you're safe?"

"Jacob, please. What are you going to do?"

"Wouldn't you like to know. How about we discuss it over dinner?"

Tera almost choked on her water. "Yeah, right. That ship has sailed."

"You've moved on already? Found another sucker to take care of you, aye?"

If things turn out the right way with Dominic, I'll be set for life. "Don't hate. As a matter of fact, I have."

"This wouldn't happen to be Dominic Jones, would it?"

"That's none of your business. But since you asked, yes. So you see we definitely can't be together anymore. I've moved on to bigger and better things."

"At least you're out of my life and out of my pockets." Jacob was doing the "Harlem Shake" inside. *The flower is growing!*

"Sorry. Don't take it personal. I know you guys are friends."

"Dominic is no friend of mine. And I hope you two are miserable together."

"Well, Jacob, I have to go. I've got to get ready to meet Mister Wonderful."

"I hope you choke on it."

"From what I heard, it's quite possible, but you and I both know I can handle any stick." Tera let out a vicious laugh.

"Goodbye, Tera."

"Good riddance, Jacob." Tera flipped her flip phone down. She was done with old money and ready to "one-two" step into new money.

Jacob heard it from the horse's mouth. She and Dominic were on their way to misery, and he couldn't be happier. *I guess I can spend time with the wife until I meet a new girlfriend to fulfill my needs. I'm glad God has a sense of humor.*

He dialed his home number to make plans to take Tricia to Rio de Janeiro the following week. He couldn't afford the sailboat he'd been eyeing for months because of his wife's generosity to his ex-girlfriend. And since he'd lost the million-dollar contract with the city, a vacation was the next best thing he could splurge on right now. Besides, he needed a vacation away from his misery and a chance to make his wife happy, before she'd learn what a son of a bitch she'd really married.

Chapter 7

Tera made an emergency hair appointment with her stylist, Chanel. She had only a short time to get her hair, nails, and feet done, find a striking dress to wear to dinner, and a matching pair of shoes. She'd waited for the day she would meet a suitor like Dominic—Rich, handsome, powerful, and somebody else's husband. Tera knew she had to use the right equipment to hook Dominic and make him her next meal ticket.

She was intrigued because of the stories she'd heard about him. His reputation preceded him. He seemed quite full of himself, but at the same time humble. He was definitely a man she'd planned to get to know better, and hopefully to set her up so plush that she wouldn't have to look for a suitor anytime soon.

"What are you grinning about?" Shaniece asked.

Tera was sitting under the hair dryer, fantasizing about all the riches Dominic could bring into her life. "I told you who I met at that benefit dinner, right?"

"Yeah. Some new direct deposit for you, right? Frankly, I don't know what you are so excited about. You guys haven't even gone out yet."

"I could feel the man is into me from the first time we met. But I won't get too cocky. This one might be a little more work than I usually put in."

"Listen to you . . . work you usually put in. Tera, I pray for you. When are you going to stop using men for your financial goals?"

"You know how I get down. What is your problem?"

"Nothing."

"Come on, spill it. I can tell something's eating at you."

Although Tera was quite self-centered, she truly cared about her cousin and her happiness. Shaniece was the only family Tera had since her mother and father deserted her.

"If I tell you, promise you won't be mad."

"Just tell me, Shaniece."

"James called me that night you went to the benefit dinner. We are back together now."

Tera almost jumped out of her seat. "Shaniece, how could you be so stupid? I hipped you to the game. Not only is James using you like some playmate, but he ain't even breaking you off with no kind of money. What is the matter with you?"

"I can't be a gold-digging whore like you, Tera. I've got feelings."

"Fuck you and your feelings, you stupid bitch. Can't you see that I'm only looking out for you? And you want to turn around and act like this towards me?"

"You just don't understand. James loves me. It's not about money or what I can get out of him."

"Girl, that man does not love you. He loves his penis. He would tell any other girl the same dribble he's telling you, just to keep her country-bumpkin, naive tail underneath him. Watch, I'm going to show you what kind of man James really is."

"You're wrong, Tera. He is going to leave his wife, you'll see."

Tera tuned Shaniece out. She had bigger fish to fry. She would deal with her cousin's drama another time. Her mood had to be right to have dinner with Mr. Jones.

The car Dominic promised to pick Tera up arrived exactly at eight p.m. She took one last look at herself in the mirror and decided she was up to par to meet Mr. Jones. She wore a thigh-high-split, fitted, navy-blue strapless dress covered with rhinestones. Her three-inch "come-fuck-me" heels gave her five-foot-three frame a little more height. Tera always wore clothes that hugged her size-six shape and tantalized her assets. Her hair was pulled back into a Chinese bun clipped with a rhinestone barrette. Her hair stylist did an amazing job with her hair and Tera looked gorgeous.

Although she looked flawless, she was still a little nervous underneath.

She wanted Dominic so bad. It took everything she had not to call him that night she'd met him. But her rules were her religion, so she waited until the right time to lay her man trap. *This is it. Don't blow it.* She kissed her reflection and stepped out to meet her prize.

The driver opened the car door to the Lincoln Town Car and tilted his hat to Ms. Larou. When Tera stepped in, she was disappointed not to see Dominic waiting inside. "Where is Mr. Jones?"

"I was instructed to pick you up. Where Mr. Jones is, I do not know."

"Where are you taking me?"

"Downtown Boston."

"Where in downtown Boston?"

"12355 Tremont Street."

Tera grew impatient. Where was Dominic taking her, and why wasn't he riding with her there? She'd planned to begin her seduction on the way to dinner. Now she would have to rethink her plan.

They arrived at a apartment skyline setoff from downtown. The sign in the front said *Dawson's Place*. The building was being remodeled and appeared vacant. Tera grew even more impatient and annoyed because she didn't think she was going to get the chance to seduce Dominic over dinner now. She didn't even know if they were having dinner any more.

The driver opened the door and let Tera out.

"Where am I supposed to go now?"

"In that building. I was instructed to see that you made it to this location. I'll be waiting for you out here when you're ready to go."

"Fine," Tera said with an attitude. Why was the driver being so secretive? Did he really not know what was going on?

Once inside, Tera noticed a glowing light coming from behind one of the apartment doors. She opened it and was delighted. Dominic sat at a dinner table for two waiting for her arrival. The room was lit with candles, and music began to play.

Dominic stood up and ushered Tera to her seat. "So glad you could join me."

"Where are we? I thought you said we were going out to dinner?"

"You assumed a restaurant, did you not?"

"I suppose."

"This is better than a restaurant. I'm making you dinner. I own this building. In the summer it should be finished. I named it after my daughter."

"Great. More apartments downtown. What an original idea."

Dominic grinned. "You have a sense of humor on you, I see. Let me pour you some wine."

Tera held up her glass and let Dominic serve her.

The dinner was impressive. Lamb chops with mashed potatoes and gravy and a side of string beans. The dessert was chocolate-covered strawberries over a shortcake with whipped cream on top.

"You have all my favorites here. Strawberries, chocolates, whipped cream, and champagne."

Dominic grinned as his manhood began to rise. He was horny from the moment Tera walked in wearing that sexy dress. To say she turned him on was an understatement.

"Enjoying the meal?"

"Especially dessert." Tera grinned seductively.

"Would you like to dance?"

"Love to."

Dominic stood and reached for Tera's hand. They danced

to the soft instrumental music from the CD player Dominic had bought, their bodies swaying together closely, as if they couldn't bear being apart.

He whispered, "So tell me your dreams, Ms. Larou."

"I could show you better than I could tell you."

Dominic looked into her hazel eyes. "You are beautiful. Where did you get those eyes?"

"My parents, silly."

"Do you look just like your mother?"

Tera couldn't bear to go there. "What is it that you do exactly?"

"Businesses seek my consult when their computer systems go awry."

"So you are a computer genius then?"

"In so many words. I've been doing this for a long time. Started from scratch. And now I own my own consulting company that is well-renowned for its reputation to debug any computer system."

"That must be very profitable."

"It is indeed. And what about you? What do you do?"

"I'm an independent asset broker, specializing in acquisitions."

"Sounds interesting. Does it keep you busy?"

"Depends on the client. Why?"

"I'm not going to front. I find you smart, attractive, and interesting. I would like to see more of you."

"Maybe that can be arranged."

"Maybe? Why maybe?"

"Because you haven't kissed me yet."

Signaled by his cue, Dominic held Tera in a passionate

kiss, which to her seemed to last forever. He began to rub her behind.

She held him tightly.

He caressed her breast as he tongued her deeper.

She moaned and placed her hand on his bulge.

Dominic didn't hesitate. He lifted Tera up into his arms and slammed her back against the wall. He began to undress himself as Tera moaned for him to be inside her.

She slid down her dress and kneeled to pleasure him more. She took Dominic in her mouth and moved in a rhythmic pattern, sucking the life out of him.

Dominic tried to resist his explosion as he grabbed Tera's hair.

When she tea-bagged him, he almost erupted.

He pulled her up and turned her around. He entered her from behind, doggy-style, against the wall, grabbing her breasts.

Tera moaned in excitement, as his penis hit all her spots. She was loving every minute of it. *He's so well endowed.* Tera pulled away, and Dominic almost lost his mind. "I want to ride you," she whispered.

Dominic lay on the floor. "I'm yours."

Tera hopped on him like a jockey and began to ride him until they both came, her body collapsing on his as her legs convulsed.

They napped for an hour, then got up, got dressed, and left their love nest. The driver was waiting to take Tera home as promised.

Dominic kissed her good night. "Dinner tomorrow?"

"We'll see. I don't know what my schedule looks like for tomorrow," Tera lied, trying to tease him.

"I want to see you tomorrow, so I will see you tomorrow, sweetness. I'll give you a call." He kissed her again. "Good night." Then he walked down the street to his parked car.

Tera watched him as the driver pulled away. She was doing a belly dance inside. Never in her wildest dreams did she think she would meet a man like Dominic, who satisfied her sexually and financially. She figured the two just didn't go together. One thing was clear. She was never going to let this suitor go.

Chapter 8

In Dominic's mind his affair with Tera was the perfect relationship. She was very understanding and easy to please when it came to their arrangement. He enjoyed fucking her brains out four times a week at their spot, and Tera never complained about the time they spent together or the fact that he had a family.

Renovations for Dawson's Place continued, but Dominic had their penthouse apartment finished in six weeks. He grew tired of bending Tera over and working his knees on the unfinished floor of the first-floor apartment at Dawson's Place.

Their love nest was the perfect hideout. During the night, no one was around and they could carry on until the early morning. Which they often did. It wasn't like Dominic was afraid that Donna would hire a private detective or anything, but rumors always bent her ear, and he didn't want to get careless. He knew Donna was loyal and faithful to him anyway, and would never leave him, no matter what she heard.

So it was settled. Tera was Dominic's new girlfriend, and he longed to be with her every chance he got.

"Baby, my car broke down," Tera said. "Can I borrow yours?"

Dominic was at work closing on another overseas deal. He didn't like to be interrupted. "What's the matter with your car?"

"I don't know. But I know I'm going to miss my salon appointment if I don't get there soon."

Tera shopped almost everyday and made trips to the beauty salon and nail salon twice a week. She'd told Dominic that she wanted to keep him happy by looking better every time he saw her.

"I'm busy working right now. Reschedule your appointment. Don't worry, I'll take care of it."

"But you know I have to look especially nice for you tonight, baby. You remember how good I looked in Acapulco, right?"

"I couldn't keep my hands off you." Dominic reminisced. He enjoyed weekend getaways with his girlfriend, often whisking her off to Jamaica or Mexico at a moment's notice.

"All right then. I have to keep myself up for you. Don't you like that?"

"Yes. Look, I said, 'Don't worry, I'll take care of it.' Don't I always?"

"You don't mind, do you? Because—"

"Because what? Haven't I made all your dreams come true as promised, baby?"

"Yes, you have."

"And don't I take care of you and pay all your bills, plus give you anything you ask for?"

"Yes, baby."

"Okay. I said I'd take care of it. Now I'll see you tonight. And wear something that's easy to take off."

"Yes, baby."

"I'll meet you at your house tonight. What's the address again?"

Tera gave Dominic the requested information and almost soaked her sofa at the thought of him coming inside her domain.

"See you at your house tonight, baby."

Keeping Tera up was no big deal to Dominic. In fact that's how he liked his women. Totally dependent on him for survival.

Later that night he showed up at her Brookline condo with a brand-new Mercedes-Benz CLK coupe.

Tera was burning with excitement. "Is this for me?"

"You don't ever have to borrow anything from me. I'd rather give it to you."

Tera showed her gratitude by giving Dominic the best sex ever that night.

During their three-month affair, Dominic was more relaxed and contented. He believed he was a better father, husband, and businessman, because he had the best girlfriend ever. They were happy.

But they were the only ones. Donna was growing sick of her teenage daughter and wanted her husband to back her up on discipline. Instead, Dominic brushed off her concerns and continued to baby Dawson the best way he could and let Donna deal with her attitude.

He told Donna, "It's a part of growing up. As long as she does well in school and don't let any boys into her pants I'm happy." The thought of his daughter having sex sickened him.

Dawson, although in every aspect a bratty teen, respected her father and listened to him. Besides, she knew she wouldn't find another man like her father to love her the way he did, so teenage boys were a waste of her time. She would flirt with them, but for the most part she had her nose so far in the air, she could smell God. She gave her mother a hard time, though, always rolling her eyes and trying her patience.

To Donna it was one more thing she couldn't handle. She fought depression and her inner demons every day. Having her husband off on business trips every other weekend didn't help her sanity either. She wondered how long she would be able to keep up appearances or deal with life if her Prozac stopped working. Happiness seemed so far away for her, dealing with her husband's so-called business trips, and her daughter's admiration for him and loathing for her. Her life might've seemed sweet, but on the inside she was crying.

Since Dominic was due back Sunday from another one of his business trips, Donna wanted to have a nice dinner for him. She invited Jacob and Tricia and made filet mignon and stuffed lobster tails. The kitchen was one of Donna's sanctuaries. Church was another. She would sing and dance in the sweet smell of her dinner cooking as she enjoyed her two loves, dancing and eating. She enjoyed always having dinner on the table for her family and took pride in all her meals. She'd learned early from her grandmother, who'd passed it down to her mother, how important it is for a woman to know what she's doing in the kitchen, not just the bedroom.

As she sang and danced to Whitney's Houston's "I Wanna Dance with Somebody," the house phone rang. She answered, "Hello."

"Hey, baby. How's the most beautiful woman in the world doing?"

"Good. How was your trip?"

"Very productive. So productive that I've got a ton of work to do tonight at the office."

"What? I'm making dinner, and I invited Tricia and Jacob over."

"Oh darn, I'm going to have to miss a dinner with the Evans. I'm so crushed. Can't we do it another time? Like never?"

"Very funny. I haven't seen you in so long. Not to mention, the pastor at our church asked me if everything was all right, seeing how he hasn't seen you at church in the past four weeks."

"It's business, honey. I've got to provide for my family. You like how we live, don't you?"

"Yes, but you know that doesn't matter to me, if I don't have you. If Dawson doesn't have her father—"

Dominic cut his wife off, not really feeling the guilt trip thing. "Donna, I have to do what I've got to do to keep this family together, and you have to do what you have to do . . . like being an understanding wife. You know I work hard."

"I know, but—"

"But nothing. Stop caring what everyone thinks. Besides, I donate so much money to the church, the pastor should be pulling his nose out of your ass, instead of putting it in our business."

"Don't talk like that. It's just . . ."

"It's just what?"

"I miss you. Dawson misses you. I would like to spend more time with—" Sensing she didn't have her husband's full attention, she said, "Dominic, are you listening?"

"What? Yeah, I heard you. I'll do my best. I should be home around midnight."

"Midnight? Dominic, we need to talk."

"I can't right now. I'm on my way to the office."

Donna heard a funny sound, like Dominic was sipping on a Slurpee. "What's that noise?"

"What noise?"

"Are you drinking something?"

"Yeah. Look, I'll call you later. Love you."

"Dominic, wait."

"I've got to go."

"I can't remember the last time I saw your penis."

"What did you say?"

"I'm sorry. Something just came over me. I miss you, and I want to make love to you."

"Okay, baby. I'll be home later. Love you."

"I love you too," Donna said. She wasn't sure that he was being truthful with her. She missed him. They hadn't made love in almost a month.

She shook off feelings that he was being unfaithful and continued to prepare dinner. Unable to handle anything else on her plate, she wasn't ready to face the truth about her marriage.

Dawson came downstairs with her headphones attached to her iPod, jamming to Destiny's Child's latest CD.

Donna signaled for her to turn it off.

"What's up?" Dawson said.

"I need you to reset the dinning room table. Your father won't be joining us."

"What else is new?"

"He's on a business trip."

"Whatever. Since Dad isn't going to be here, I don't see why I have to suffer through dinner with your friends."

"Excuse me?"

Dawson rolled her eyes at her mother and, without an ounce of concern, walked out of the kitchen and back up to her room.

Donna fought the temptation to strangle her daughter with her headphones. *Lord, give me strength. Will this ever end?*

Meanwhile, Dominic was enjoying the pleasure Tera was bringing him. She stroked his penis with her tongue like she was licking an ice cream cone. He'd never had it so good.

They'd missed their flight earlier that morning, because of the wild and passionate lovemaking the night before. Hungover from sex, they couldn't drag themselves out of bed to make it to LAX. They spent the weekend in Los Angeles. He took her shopping in Beverly Hills during the day, and during the night they did what they did best—sex each other to sleep.

Tera had no plans of doing anyone ever again the way she did Dominic. He had her hypnotized.

As for Dominic, he enjoyed every minute of the ride.

Chapter 9

"Can you turn up the AC? I'm hot," Dawson whined.

"I'll do you one better." Donna pressed the button to let the top down on her Mercedes-Benz convertible. The Jones women were on their way to the usual Saturday routine—hair appointment, shopping, and then an early dinner at Jam's, Donna's best friend, Jamila's, soul food restaurant.

Donna enjoyed spending quality time with her daughter, so they could talk and she could get in her business.

"Mom, I need to find a dress to wear to Fiona's party next Saturday. I'm hoping they have something in bebe."

"I don't like you shopping in that store. Those clothes are too grown up for you."

"Everyone my age is wearing that."

"So if everyone was to drop off a cliff, would you too?"

"Oh forget it. You always overdramatize everything. It's just a freaking store."

"Whose Fiona again?"

"The varsity cheerleading captain. She's throwing an

end-of-the-year party for the squad, and the basketball and football teams. I think she's going to announce the captains for next year. I hope I make it."

"It's your first year, sweetie. You're only going to be a junior next year."

"Hello—earth to Donna—the varsity captain is like the best position I could be in, especially if I'm going to be a junior next year. I kicked ass on that squad this year with my back handsprings, mounts, and splits. I should be captain next year, point-blank. The rest of those girls are sloppy seconds."

"Don't get cute, Dawson Dominique Jones. You aren't too old for me to tear up that backside." Donna glanced over at her daughter with serious-business eyes. "Watch your mouth. Talk like a lady, do you hear me?"

"Yes, Mother." Dawson folded her arms and rolled her eyes.

"I'm just saying, there are more important things than cheerleading. Next year you should be thinking about college and maintaining a four point O grade average. The PSATs are this fall. There will be recruiters from Ivy League school as well. College is much more competitive than cheerleading."

"All right, Mom, I get it. Can't a girl have a little fun?"

"Life isn't all fun and games, missy. You have to make the right choices in life because you can't go back and fix them later."

"Here we go. I know, I know already. Geesh! Cool it with the speech. I've heard it a million times already—Just books, smarts, and college. No booze, boys, or drugs— I've got it."

"I can nag you if I want. I've only got two more years before you're off to college and doing exciting things with your life."

"Who says I want to go to college? I might want to be an actress or musician or model."

"Dawson, I'll take all your credit cards now if I hear that foolishness. You're going to college. You can be anything, but you need the education first."

"Mom, you're so old-school. You can do well without going to college. Look at P. Diddy."

"Look at your father, not some hip-hop mogul. Your father worked his behind off in school, landed a job with the elite in his industry, and now has his own Fortune 500 Company. He should be your role model."

"Whatever."

"I'm serious. Education gives you options . . . so many opportunities. Plus you will meet exciting new people." Donna sighed. "I just want you to have that experience. Your choices will be endless. You will be able to write your own ticket and not have to latch on to anyone for his or her success. *You'll* be the success."

"Okay, Mom. Dang! You talk like it's the only way. Maybe I just want to marry rich, you know, be a housewife like you. It seems a lot easier than having to really work."

Donna pulled the car off the road and turned the music down. "Now you listen to me like you never could hear before. My life isn't the life I want you to have. You are going to be something. Not just anything, but a woman who carries so much grace, intelligence, and beauty that the very thought of you inspires great things. You will not just be some man's wife. You will be your own woman, strong and indestructible. You have no idea how much your father had to struggle to get where he is, and you have no clue what it took for me to watch him rise as I took care of home. But that was my path, my choice. And I didn't give up my dreams of becoming a dancer in that same limelight that you dream of, to have my only daughter become just a devoted, Martha-Stewart-*Living* housewife. I've sacrificed a lot for this family because I love you and Dominic more than I love myself. And that's why it's important for you to understand the road that has been laid before your feet. You're a princess, Dawson, and you deserve better than to be the background of some man's success. You will be your own woman, so help me God, if it kills me."

Dawson had chills up her spine and goose bumps on her arms. She felt like crying but held back tears. She admired her mother more than she let on and couldn't understand, until now, why her mother didn't pursue her dreams of becoming a dancer. Dawson would gawk over her mother's photographs when she was a dancer and pray that she would inherit the same grace and beauty as her mother. Dawson used to get frustrated with her mother's constant nagging, but she better understood now why her mother was so adamant that she pursue her own dreams.

"Okay, Mom, I get it. I'm going to college."

Donna kissed her daughter's hand. "Yes, my lady, you sure are."

Donna didn't mean to go off on a tangent like that with Dawson, but she desperately wanted her daughter to get away from home. More importantly, get away from her father and her.

In public, Donna made their life seem so enviable. Perfect, wealthy, intelligent husband, living in a mansion, everyone in town knew them and sucked up to them. The Joneses basically could do or have anything they damn well pleased. But that was the problem. Dominic had and did everything, and everyone he pleased.

She never imagined her life would turn out like this. She wanted to be a ballet dancer and choreographer. In college she was part of the Turps, a ballet and expressive dance troupe. One hundred and thirty-five pounds and a size seven, she loved to dance and couldn't wait to study at Juilliard or some other famous dance school, even though her parents wanted her to be a pediatrician. Donna wanted to live in the limelight and enjoyed it when the audience applauded and gave her a standing ovation. She loved to express her feelings through dance, and the sound of music made her come alive inside.

Nothing in life seemed better than dancing, until she met and fell in love with Dominic. They married after college, against Donna's parents' wishes, and moved to Boston, where Dominic landed a job.

A month later when Donna found out she was pregnant, the Joneses couldn't have been happier. Until tragedy took over their life. Donna's heart saddened as she remembered a time when life for Dominic and her had so much promise. They had been married a couple of months and . . .

Chapter 10

A twenty-two-year-old Donna put a wooden board against the broken glass in the window of the one-bedroom apartment she and Dominic shared. It was the middle of winter. Their slumlord, as Dominic called him, promised to have it fixed six months earlier. Although their apartment was tiny, it didn't hold any heat, and the gas prices in Boston were ridiculous.

Donna wanted desperately to ask her parents for money, but Dominic, up for another promotion at his job after only being there six months, wouldn't hear of it. He bargained with her to hold on until he got his promotion. Then they would leave this poor house and be "moving on up" like George and Weezy.

Dominic tickled Donna's already oversized belly. "What has your Momma been feeding you?"

Donna tried to stop laughing. Since her pregnancy, she was ticklish all over. "Stop. You're going to make me pee on myself."

"Okay, okay." He pulled out the Chinese food restaurant menu. "What do you want, chicken wings or chicken fingers?"

"I told you we have leftover spaghetti. We shouldn't be spending unnecessary money. We have a baby coming, you know."

Dominic ignored her and kept reading the menu.

"Dominic, I'm serious. Plus if you get that new promotion, she can go to daycare, and I can go to dancing school."

Dominic stopped perusing the menu. "She who? Who says it's going to be a girl? I think you've got a little Dominic inside there, baby." He tried to tickle her again.

Donna pulled away. "I mean it. I have plans after the baby is born. I want to pursue my dreams too."

"What plans? Baby, your only responsibility will be to raise our children and be a good wife. You know, take care of our home."

"But I love dancing. I could be a famous choreographer, you know. Maybe for Janet Jackson or even Michael Jackson."

"Yeah, right. Sweetie, trust me, if everything works out the way I plan, in a few years the Jacksons will be working for us."

"I want to be a choreographer, Dominic. I didn't go to college to be your wife."

"What about our kids? Don't you want to be a mother to them?"

"I can work too."

"No. I know what it's like not to have a mother around. I don't want that for my children."

"Both my parents worked."

"We're not your parents."

"You knew I wanted to attend Juilliard before we got married."

"And then you got pregnant. Your priorities changed."

"Yeah, but I still can go to dance school and be your wife and a mother to our children."

"That's ridiculous. I don't want you working. I love you so much that I would do anything for you. Just let me take care of our family."

"But what about my dreams?"

"Okay, maybe after we have two more children. By the time they're old enough to go to school, then you can pursue your dreams. In the meantime, volunteer or teach dance class or something."

Donna began to think.

"And after that, then maybe I can buy you your own dance school."

Donna hugged Dominic so hard, he could hardly breathe. "You promise?"

"Yes, I promise."

"Kiss me."

Dominic held his wife close and kissed her passionately.

Donna felt like she was the luckiest woman in the world to have such a wonderful husband.

"Mom, why are you crying?" Dawson asked. "I said I would go to school."

"I know, honey. I just get emotional sometimes, you know me." Donna was deep in thought and didn't realize she had begun to cry. She tried to be strong for her only child, but sometimes her emotions got the better of her.

Dawson shrugged. True, her mother cried at the drop of a hat, but she could never understand why she was so sensitive and emotional. That was one thing she didn't want to inherit. What Dawson didn't know was the pain her mother carried with her.

Donna parked the car by the Filene's garage at the Galleria Mall. She checked her mirror to fix her makeup and realized what a mess she was. Her energy was so low. Old wounds were surfacing, and Donna needed to pull it together if she was going to be able to put up her usual picture-perfect image. She popped open her pill bottle and took an extra dose of Prozac, but a growing sting would not leave her heart as she and Dawson shopped at the Mall.

"Mom, I'm going to bebe. I'll meet you at the food court or something." Dawson could recognize her mother's mood shift and didn't like being anywhere near her when that happened.

Not recalling her previous objection to bebe, Donna waved her daughter off and became fixated on a woman bouncing her baby boy on her lap.

Through the worst snowstorm of 1990, Dominic rushed Donna to the hospital. Her water had broken, and she was in agonizing pain.

"Can't you go any faster, I'm dying?"

"Stay focused, baby. You're not dying. Remember to breathe. Hold my hand."

Donna grabbed for her husband's hand, and the car swerved as Dominic grimaced in unison with his wife's pain.

"I said hold my hand, not break it."

"Watch the road! I'm dying. I just know I'm dying. Hurry UP!"

As Dominic drove feverishly through the messy roads, Donna moaned and screamed louder. Dominic was about to lose his mind. He wasn't afraid, though. He was willing to do anything to keep his family safe. He drove through the snow like he was rafting through wild river terrain.

As soon as they got there, hospital attendants rushed Donna into a Labor and Delivery room.

Hours went by as she moaned and moaned, "I can't take this pain. I need something." She wasn't handling second-stage labor well.

The nurse kept trying to make her comfortable, but Donna wouldn't relax. She would push and breathe, and she wasn't even two centimeters dilated. Finally, the nurse caved, and the anesthesiologist gave Donna an epidural.

Donna felt like she was higher than she was when she experimented with marijuana in high school. Her labor slowed. She dilated to four centimeters in eight hours. The doctor was afraid she wouldn't progress, so he ordered for the nurse to give her Pitocin, to speed up the labor process.

Two hours later, Donna pushed one final time.

"Oh shit!" Dominic yelled. "I can see the head."

Donna let out a loud moan, and slippery slide, their baby came flying out.

"It's a girl," the doctor yelled.

Dominic kissed Donna with pure admiration for what she'd just gone through.

"Let me see her," Donna said.

The doctor placed the baby on her chest, and they fell in

love at first sight. "Would you like to cut the cord?" he asked Dominic, handing him the scissors..

Dominic proudly nodded. "She's beautiful." He kissed his baby, covered in his wife's fluids, on her forehead. "I love you. Daddy will always take care of his girls."

Donna smiled up at her husband, but her eyes started to roll into the back of her head.

"She doesn't look so good, Doctor," Dominic said. "What's the matter?"

"Her BP is sixty over 35, Doctor," the nurse yelled. "She's hemorrhaging."

The doctor started to yell out orders, "Grab the crash cart. Open her IV fluids wider. Get me two point five milligrams of Methergine stat!"

Frightened and confused, Dominic asked, "What's going on?"

The nurse grabbed their baby, and another nurse came running in and escorted Dominic out.

"What's going on?"

"Your wife is bleeding. We need to stabilize her. Please wait out here, and we will come out to you as soon as we know something."

"As soon as you know something?" Dominic's heart dropped.

The nurse closed the labor room door and left him with the dread in his soul.

Hours later the doctor came out and explained that they had to perform an emergency hysterectomy to save Donna's life. "She's stable now and awake. You can go and see her."

"A hyster*what*? What does that mean?"

"We needed to remove her uterus to stop the bleeding. I'm sorry."

Dominic felt a lump in his throat. "So she can't have any more children?"

"I'm sorry."

"Does she know?"

"I just finished going over it with her. You should go in there."

Dominic was at a loss. "What should I say?"

"Just go to her."

Dominic didn't know what Donna was feeling, but he couldn't imagine it was any easier for her. He entered the room, unsure of what he was walking into. He came upon a tearful, withdrawn Donna. She didn't even look at him.

Then it hit him. The woman he knew a short while ago was gone. It was as if, in saving her life, the doctors killed something inside her.

Dominic couldn't think of anything to say. Too many thoughts ran through his mind. *Thank you for sparing her. But how could you take this away from her? From us? Thank you for our healthy baby. Things will never be the same.* Dominic kissed his wife and crawled into her bed to hold her tight. He felt so sorry for them but, at the same time, so grateful.

Donna still wouldn't look at him. She kept crying and staring off into the room, rocking herself back and forth as Dominic hung on, unwilling to let go.

Donna carried this sadness inside her heart, but no one would ever know it.

She window-shopped at the mall, not really in the mood to purchase anything. As agreed, she looked for Dawson at the food court. *Lord knows, I have no business eating anything.*

Donna was in such a weird place, so far from what she dreamed of being and who she really wanted to be.

After giving birth, she sank deep into postpartum depression. It got to the point where she used food as her savior and blamed herself for Dominic's wondering ways because she had gotten fat. Or maybe it was the guilt that haunted her about losing her womb, ruining their chance of having any more children. If it weren't for Jamila, who watched her slowly deteriorate after giving birth to Dawson, Donna wouldn't have gone to a therapist to work out her problems. Now Prozac and therapy kept her head somewhat clear from the anguish she was feeling inside.

She waited patiently for her daughter at the food court. *Where the hell is Dawson? That girl could shop all day if she wanted to.*

Although she blamed it mostly on Dominic for their daughter being so spoiled, Donna knew she had a hand in it as well. Because of her mood instability, she neglected Dawson when she was a baby. She didn't have the energy to take care of Dawson or herself, so Dominic took care of them both.

After she got treatment, she felt like she'd been a horrible mother when Dawson was younger and was now overcompensating. Since she couldn't focus on herself, she decided to focus on Dominic and Dawson, forgetting about her own goals. If she could, she would rewind time to pursue her goals and start a family later. But Donna couldn't go back. Her life was what it was, and she would be damned if that would be Dawson's.

Chapter 11

Jam's was packed. There was at least an hour-and-a-half wait for a table. Saturday evening was its busiest night because the restaurant was located in the heart of downtown. All the college students, downtown shoppers, and daters flowed through the place because of its signature soul food and live band.

Tera waited patiently with James for their table, but she was eager to get the night over with. "Let's just go somewhere else."

"Naw, baby. Our table will be ready soon. My man's girl owns this place."

"I think we can get to know each other a little better if we were alone," Tera said, stroking his goatee.

James was very surprised when Tera called him. He'd wanted to tap that ass ever since Shaniece introduced them and didn't think a classy chick like Tera would be interested in a hard-working construction company owner like himself. And he was right.

Tera had ulterior motives—Get James in bed, so she could prove to Shaniece he would never leave his wife, let alone be faithful to her. It was the only way she was sure her silly cousin would get rid of this puppy dog. She wanted better things for her cousin. After trying to reason with her, it was time for drastic measures. After all, James wasn't even in her league. Yeah, he had his own company, but he couldn't hold a candle to Dom. That's what Tera nicknamed Dominic. James shouldn't even be able to breathe the same air as Dom, Tera believed.

At any rate, if things kept going the way she'd planned, she would never have to find another suitor ever again. Her electronic address book was getting full anyway, and she couldn't think of a wealthier suitor than Dom. Over the last three months, he'd showered her with so many gifts that she never wanted to date someone out of his tax bracket ever again. She figured she could be Dom's girlfriend forever, and he could be her full-time job. She just needed to do this one thing for her cousin, and Dom would be all she'd ever need.

Tera whispered in James's ear, "Let's get out of here, and you can take me some place quiet."

James knew exactly what that meant and was all too ready to oblige, but then the hostess signaled that their table was ready.

Before James could move, the Jones women walked in and smiled at the hostess, who without stuttering, said, "Right this way, Mrs. Jones."

James got up and demanded to speak to the owner, since the hostess just gave away their table after he'd waited for damn near an hour.

Tera's attention was fixated on Mrs. Jones. *Could it be?*

She watched as Jamila hugged Mrs. Jones and said, "You look fierce, girl. Dawson, you are getting so grown."

"*Too* grown," Donna replied, as the women enjoyed their sisterhood embrace.

It was confirmed. That was Dominic's wife and only daughter. Tera felt a sudden urge to get a closer look at her boyfriend's wife. She excused herself from James and followed Donna to the restroom. Pretending to fix her makeup, she waited patiently for her to come out of the stall to get a closer look. Jealously flew through her veins as she secretly stared at Donna coming toward the sink.

As always Donna was dressed to the nines, wearing clothes that flattered her shape. For a plus-size woman, Donna had it going on, and looked like she could compete with any size-two bulimic model. Her purple blazer covered her abdominal rolls and revealed just the right amount of cleavage. She wore dark blue denim capris and purple Manolo Blahnik strap-heeled sandals. Donna's ice gleamed from head to ankle as she wore her diamond platinum studs, tennis bracelet, platinum wedding ring and band, and her diamond-studded ankle bracelet.

As Donna fixed her lips and played with her shoulder-length, bone-straight black hair, she noticed Tera's envious stares. "Have we met?" Donna asked, noticing Tera was still checking her out.

"I don't think so. Hey, would you happen to have a tampon? Silly flow snuck up on me?"

"Sorry, sweetie, I don't. I have no use for them."

A bit puzzled, Tera replied, "I'm sorry. You look way too young to have hit menopause." *Dom's wife is an old lady.*

Donna smiled. "Goodness no, I had a hysterectomy. I'm too young for menopause, girl."

Tera laughed an embarrassed deceitful laugh. "I'm sorry. Didn't mean to get in your business. Thanks anyway. Hey, by the way, your sandals are hot. Manolo?"

"Yeah, my husband knows I love shoes. He bought these for me while he was on a business trip in New York. I can't believe he actually bought something I like." Donna smiled.

Tera's green-eyed monster was break-dancing in her head. "Oh, how sweet of him."

"I know. Dominic can be such a ham when he wants to be."

"I can imagine." *More than you can imagine, bitch.*

"Well, I hope you find what you need, girl. I keep telling my girl to put a machine in here, but she hasn't yet."

"Your friend works here?"

"She owns this place. I bring my daughter in here every Saturday. It's our thing. My girl always has a table for us, no matter how long someone's been waiting. I guess that's unfair for other people, but it's good to have friends."

"That, it is." Tera forced a smile.

"Well, nice meeting you . . ."

"Tera. My name is Tera. And yours?"

"Donna."

"Nice to meet you, Donna. Take care."

Tera stormed out of the restroom and found James at a corner table that he'd bargained for with Jamila. "I'm ready to go."

"I just sat down. I figured we could have some dinner and later have dessert." James grinned.

After running into Dom's bitch-wife, Tera wanted to leave,

but decided to carry on with her "get-James-out-of-her-cousin's-life" mission. "Sweetheart, let me put it to you like this—The only thing I've got an appetite for is you. So if you want some collard greens and fried chicken, instead of me fucking the taste out your mouth, then I've got to leave you with your fried chicken."

On that note, James quickly hurried Tera out of the restaurant and to the nearest hotel.

Fucking James was so easy because Tera could allow herself to become numb when she was with him, just like with all her other suitors. Except for Dominic.

Later that night, Tera couldn't sleep because she wanted to be next to Dominic. She wanted him to hold her and surprise her by buying her expensive sandals and shit, instead of giving her a ball of cash to buy whatever. She tried to shake those ridiculous feelings off and stick with her religion.

Who gives a fuck about the wife or what he buys her? My position is much sweeter. Silly housewife, she doesn't have a clue of the good loving Dom receives over here. He thinks about me all the time, even when he is having sex with you.

Tera tried to let her imaginary conversation with Donna sink in, but she couldn't abandon the growing shadow upon her thoughts. *Why do you even care?*

A puzzled Tera tossed and turned throughout the night. For the first time in her "girlfriend career," she wished she were Donna. She wished she were Dominic's wife.

Chapter 12

"Good morning, Mr. Jones. You have a one o'clock, a two o'clock, and an evening dinner party tonight at seven," Monique said, trying to keep her boss up to speed.

"A dinner party? With who? Where?"

"At your house. It's your wife's birthday and you arranged for a caterer and band to be at your home by 5:30 p.m."

"That's right. Shoot, I didn't buy her anything yet."

"That's taken care of. I've already sent her one hundred roses."

"That's my girl. What about a note or a card with it?"

"One hundred roses, for one hundred times to say I love you."

"Nice touch. I knew there was a reason I gave you a raise."

Monique giggled. "That wasn't the only reason."

Dominic tried to clear his mind. Thoughts of smacking her behind while ramming his penis into her vagina doggy-style hounded him. "Anything else for me?"

"Yeah, some woman who says she's your asset advisor or something is here to see you."

Dominic grinned. "Send her in."

Tera walked in dressed in a trench business jacket and wearing eyeglasses. Her hair was pinned up and pulled back into a bun, and she was wearing the diamond hoop earrings he'd bought for her.

"Hello."

Tera smiled. "Hello yourself." She pushed Dominic back into his chair and revealed she was only wearing a pink lace thong teddy with matching pink thigh-high stockings.

Dominic immediately rose to the occasion at his girlfriend's erotic gesture. Tera proved to be the best girlfriend yet. She was freaky as hell and she gave it to him just how he liked it, raw and nasty. She understood him and wasn't a nag. "I wanna see you later," he told her.

"How about around eight?"

"That sounds good. Oh wait, I forgot I've got something to do tonight. How about tomorrow?"

Is he blowing me off? "Well, what do you have to do that you can't come by later on tonight?"

Dominic kissed her lips, then he held up her chin and said, "What, when, why? You know I don't answer to that."

Tera pouted. "It's just . . . I wanted to see you later and finish what we started today." She began to kiss his neck, then his chest, then his navel and then—

"Tera, baby, wait. Later. I'll try to see you later. I've got work to do."

"Promise?" Tera whined.

"Yeah, whatever." He kissed her again and got dressed. *Guess I spoke too soon. So much for not being a nag.*

Dominic almost didn't make it home in time because his secretary took a two-hour lunch and didn't get the gift he wanted for Donna. *If Monique didn't give such good head, I'd have to fire her ass.* He had to backtrack to the jewelry store to pick up an emerald studded diamond necklace.

Dawson greeted him at the door when he got home, "Daddy, I knew you'd forget."

"I didn't forget. I had to pick up something special for your mom."

"Yeah, right." Dawson laughed. "You forgot."

Dominic grabbed and hugged his daughter and then began to tickle her.

Donna walked in on their embrace and just watched. She loved how they adored each other.

Looking up, Dominic greeted his wife by singing in a silly off-key voice, "Happy birthday to you. Happy birt-daaaaaaaaaaaayyyy—"

Donna covered her ears. "Please stop. I can't take it." She grinned.

"Did you get my roses?"

"Yes, they were beautiful. I especially loved the card."

"You deserve it. What do you say?"

"I love you." Donna kissed and held him in a genuine embrace.

Dominic kissed her back. "You better love me."

Feeling lucky she had two parents that loved each other so much, Dawson looked on as her parents enjoyed each other.

There was a time when Donna was all Dominic needed. As he hugged his wife, he reminisced. *My, my, my. How things have changed.*

* * *

LL Cool J's song blasted through the radio: "I take a muscle-bound man and put his face in the sand . . . I'm bad."

Dominic and his college groupies hung around him as he did the "whop." His thick gold Gucci link chain hung over his boyish chest. He wore a red adidas sweat suit and a white Kangol, with fresh white Converse sneakers. LL Cool J was his favorite rapper, next to Eric B. and Rakim. Dominic was passing out flyers to this hot off-campus party he was throwing that night. He was known as the bad boy on campus. Always throwing parties in his dorm or on campus, he knew the hottest spots in the city to go to and could get you in even if you didn't have ID. All the girls loved him, and the boys respected his game. When rumors about his father being a big-time drug dealer in the city surfaced, that only made him seem more edgy and dangerous.

"Ladies, come wearing something tight and you get in free all night," Dominic promised. The college girls blushed and giggled at one of the finest brothers at Howard University.

As his boom box pumped out the hottest songs of the year, he noticed a group of girls strolling by him, but not stopping to take his flyers. *Stuck-up chicks.* "Hey, ladies, you can't pass by me without saying a hello."

Three of the four girls smiled and said, "Hello," in unison.

Dominic stared at the fourth girl, who didn't part her lips. She was brown-skinned and styled her hair in a long black braid. He touched her braid. "What's up? How you doing?"

"I'm fine."

Dominic grinned. "I didn't ask you how you look, I asked, 'How are you doing?'"

The other girls giggled, but she didn't.

"And just who am I speaking to?"

"Dominic Jones. And you are?"

The girl rolled her eyes. "Donna Wynn."

"And where are you off to Ms. Donna?"

"We have dance practice. We're in the Turps. Have you heard of us?"

"Oh yeah. Can I come watch you practice?"

The other girls giggled again. They were creaming for him.

Donna said calmly, "It's a free country."

One of the other girls gave Donna "the look."

Donna didn't really give a damn if she came off rude to Dominic or not. "What?"

Dominic stared at Donna up and down. She was extra hot for him and he knew it. He thought she was one of the most beautiful women he'd ever seen. He had to have her. He loved that she had this innocent thing about her but with an attitude that would turn the average man away. Not Dominic, though. He secretly watched her perform during dance practice.

He finally got up the nerve to ask her out one day and after that they were inseparable.

Donna thought Dominic was so kind and gentle-hearted, a much different man than other people thought him to be. They had so much fun together, and the other students on campus were so jealous of them. They loved it, though.

After months of dating, one night as they were chilling in Dominic's D.C. apartment, Dominic was ready to take their relationship to the next level but felt it was time for Donna to know the truth. "You heard about my father, right?"

Donna acted like she didn't know what he was talking about. "What do you mean?"

"I know you heard the rumors, so I want to set the record straight, before this goes any further."

"Okay."

"My dad always taught me to be my own man and be the one writing the checks to his employees, not the other way around. He didn't want this life for me and wanted me to go to school and be an entrepreneur. I never knew my mother. She died giving birth to me, so my grandmother raised me." Dominic put his head down.

Donna rubbed his face. "Tell me, Dominic."

"I always wanted to be like my dad, but he would always beat me or punish me if I acted up at school or he caught me hanging out in the streets. It wasn't until he was murdered from some shady drug bullshit that I finally got what he was trying to teach me."

Donna continued to stroke his face as she listened.

Dominic was on the brink of tears. "I wish he could see me now."

"He can see you, baby. Why are you telling me this?"

"Because I love you, and I want you to know everything about me . . . if you really want to take it there with me."

Donna was so overwhelmed with sympathy and emotion. She felt privileged that Dominic could share this part of him. She wanted to share a part of her with him too, and they made love for the first time.

Those were the best years they'd shared before Donna gave birth. Dominic was devastated afterward. As Donna began to sink deeper into post-partum depression, he'd no-ticed a change in her mood, but was preoccupied with spoiling Dawson and climbing the corporate ladder. Donna acted like she didn't want anything to do with him. Her mood was always down, she never wanted to make love, she ignored Dawson, and Dominic couldn't take it anymore.

He made himself busy by forming a business plan to start his own company and put all his energy into building his company. After eight years of hustling, his company, Jones IT Consultants, was finally making millions in profit. Dominic moved his family out of the city to the suburbs of Milton, where they lived in their eight-bedroom mansion.

The more powerful he became in his business, the more he neglected his wife. Seeking attention from female business associates here and picking up a pretty young thing in afterwork bars became routine. Before he knew it, Dominic began to yearn for the company of other women.

After he started having affairs, he noticed Donna was getting better. He didn't attribute that to her therapy or medication, but instead to his extracurricular activities.

After a while, his wistful affairs became more involved and lengthy. Dominic found himself juggling his serial girlfriends with family life and enjoying it. His girlfriends kept him happy and therefore kept his family happy. Living a double-life became the only way to live, and Dominic wouldn't have it any other way.

Chapter 13

Monique invited Donna's closest friends to her dinner party. There was a total of six couples: Jamila and her boyfriend Dallas; Patricia and Jacob; Donna's parents, her sister Morgan and husband Deon; Dominic's grandmother and her significant other, Rufus; and Dominic's best friend, Seth and his wife Naomi.

The couples enjoyed the West Indian cuisine, which was prepared by one of Donna's favorite restaurants, Celia's. Monique had also arranged for a live band to play at the Jones's house for Donna's birthday dinner as well. Everyone was having a wonderful time.

After dinner, the couples danced to the band playing old-school hip-hop and some of Dominic's grandmother's nineteen fifties' hits.

Donna thoroughly enjoyed her birthday being surrounded by people she loved. She couldn't have asked for a better time.

The hour was getting late, and Dominic's grandmother

had to go. She gave Donna a book by Karen Quinones Miller called *Satin Doll* for her birthday. "I know how much you love books by African-American authors, so I thought you would enjoy this one especially."

"Thanks, Nana. You always know what I need."

Morgan and Deon had to get going as well. Morgan had just had a baby and couldn't stand being away from her for long. Donna's parents had traveled from Connecticut to celebrate their daughter's birthday and planned to stay at the Jones's for the night. Worn out from the drive, they couldn't hang, so they retired to their room.

Seth and Naomi also had to cut out. Naomi had a business meeting in the morning at her engineering firm. The rest of the couples enjoyed wine and played Taboo until one a.m.

"It's getting late, baby. I think we should get going," Tricia said to her husband.

"Okay, I'm ready. Happy birthday again, Donna. You don't look a day over twenty-five," Jacob said.

"You're too kind, Jacob, thanks for coming. I loved the gift. Thanks so much, you guys," Donna said to Jacob and Tricia. They'd given her a gift certificate to the spa for a one-hour massage and facial. Donna could always use some relaxing.

"Where did Dominic run off to? I wanted to say good night?" Tricia said.

"He was just here. Maybe he went to the bathroom or something. Jacob, see if you can find him, please."

Jacob nodded yes, because it was Donna's birthday and she and his wife were close friends. He only tolerated Dominic. As Jacob walked through the foyer and toward the first-floor bathroom, he heard voices coming from Dominic's office.

Dominic was on his cell phone talking. "All right, I will try to make it. I'll see what I can do."

Tera, who had been blowing up Dominic's phone all night, was growing more and more impatient with his other engagement and couldn't understand why he wasn't available to her like he'd promised. "I just don't understand why you would rather be with her than me? Does she take care of you like I do, baby?"

"Tera, look, I told you it's my wife's birthday. Frankly, I shouldn't have to explain anything to you."

"And why not? You want to see me, don't you?"

"Here we go again. I don't have time for this. Don't call me, I'll call you."

"But—"

"I mean it, Tera. I'll be over in two hours."

"Promise?"

Dominic hung up on her. Perturbed by her needy behavior, he planned to have a talk with her about her calling his cell phone so much. She knew how the game was played and couldn't understand why she was tripping.

Jacob came up on him. "Hey, man, Tricia just wanted to say good night to you."

"Hey, man, thanks for coming tonight. It meant a lot to Donna." *I wonder how long he's been standing there?*

"Yeah. I know they are close. How did you pull off this gig?" Jacob was trying to make small talk with Dominic. He'd noticed throughout the entire night that Dominic's cell phone seemed to vibrate several times, and he wanted to see if his hunch that Dominic was attempting to make a rendezvous with Tera was accurate. And if it was, his plan to set them up worked, and soon Dominic would be feeling the same lightness in his wallet that he was feeling after dealing with Tera.

"You just have to know what your wife is into, that kind of thing."

"Hey, do you remember that woman I introduced you to the night of the benefit dinner?"

Dominic pretended to think. "Nope. Can't say that I do."

"Her name was Tera Larou. She had these hazel eyes and a body like 'please, baby, don't hurt 'em.' You remember, right?"

"Naw, it still isn't ringing any bells."

"Well the thing is . . ."

Meanwhile the ladies were amidst a conversation of their own. Dallas excused himself to the bathroom as the women let the wine guide their thoughts.

"Hey, Jamila, you better make sure he's going to the bathroom. You never know with these men." Tricia laughed.

"Worry about your own husband, please. I'm not married to him no way, so I don't have the same concerns."

Donna raised her glass in the air. "Here, here."

"Girl, I know sometimes I wish me and Jacob didn't get married so soon, but other times, I know it was what I wanted and it was ultimately the best decision."

"Until he's seeing some bitch on the side," Jamila said.

"Look at us. We married very well. Our husbands take care of our families and us. We don't have to work unless we want to, and we basically have everything at our feet, but we still complain. Sometimes, I think life just wasn't meant to be easy," Donna said.

"It wasn't. And that is why I will never marry Dallas. What we have is too special to be complicated by marriage."

"Yeah, right," Donna said. "Deep down you want to marry Dallas."

"I do, but I just don't want things to change. I'm content with how they are. I don't want to have to worry about if my husband is cheating and then be conflicted about leaving him because of the vows we took. This way, if I ever find out Dallas is cheating on me, I can dump him without this sense of duty or responsibility hanging over me."

"I understand, but what about security?" Tricia asked.

"Hello—I have my own business."

"But what about love and commitment, building a family, a foundation?" Donna asked.

"We are committed to each other and we are in love. Marriage and a family would complicate that, I think."

"It gets complicated when your husband sleeps with every piece of ass in town," Donna said.

"I know, honey, but what are you suppose to do?"

"I wish I knew. I really wish I had followed my dreams and been my own woman like you, Jamila." Donna was holding back the tears.

"We choose our own paths, honey. They are laid at our feet, and we either take them or run from them. When a different path is before you, you will know which way to go." Jamila hugged her weakened friend. She too wished that Donna had made a better choice, but she was in love with Dominic and they now had a family and she had a responsibility to her family. So she understood why Donna stayed with him, even though he was unfaithful. "You know you can always count on me for anything. Give me this glass. You've had too much wine."

"Before you go, let's make a toast to the wives."

The women held up their glasses.

"May we see what we are supposed to see, be who we are supposed to be, and love who we are supposed to love. Let us be an inspiration to all wives."

"Good toast, Tricia," Jamila said. "Well, good night, my dear friends. Tell Dominic and Jacob I said goodnight. I don't know where they ran off."

Jamila collected Dallas, he said his good nights, and they left.

"I don't know what I'd do if I didn't have a friend like Jamila in my life. She has really been there for me."

"You've had a tough time, sweetie, but don't let Dominic's philandering ways get to you. Just get even."

"What do you mean?"

"I can always sense when Jacob is being unfaithful. He's always working late and he's extra nice and sweet to me. So this last time, I knew he had some girlfriend, but I wasn't sure until I met the tramp."

"Where?"

"At that benefit dinner Dominic spoke at a couple of months ago. I walked in on them out on the terrace."

"What? He had the nerve to have her there while he was there with you? I know you must have been pissed."

"Girl, I was about to lose my religion. But I counted to ten, because I didn't want to cause a scene. I walked up to them like I didn't have a clue."

"What did you do?"

"I asked who she was and she gave me some fifth-grader story. I went along with it. She said Jacob was making a contribution for one hundred thousand dollars and she was the benefactor of the scholarship or something."

"So he gave her one hundred thousand dollars?"

"Jacob wasn't going to give her anything, but I knew he wanted to buy some boat the following week. So instead of him sailing off in the sunset with another tramp, I wrote her a check and pretended I bought her scam."

"Tricia, you are crazy. What did he say afterwards?"

"What could he say? I told him how proud I was of him for choosing to donate instead of buying some silly sailboat."

Donna laughed.

"Till this day, he still looks at the picture of that boat, kicking himself in the behind for being such an idiot."

"But how do you know he still isn't seeing this woman?"

"Because he is back to being grumpy with me and spending less time at work."

They both laughed.

"Tricia, you are too much. I wouldn't have given that heifer anything. You're better than me, because I think I would've whupped somebody's ass."

"See, Donna, you have to learn to play your position. You are Dominic's wife and at the end of the day, you will always be his wife. He would never leave you because he knows you and Dawson are the only thing that he has done right in his life. Men like Dominic are little insecure boys underneath all their macho talk and wandering penis ways. They are weak. We are the strong ones, because we keep the family together. And I will be damned if I'm going to let some trollop come along and take my place. Not after all the sweat, tears, and blood, I've put into this relationship."

"So it's about you then?"

"Exactly. Stop thinking his cheating is about you. It's about his need to fulfill his inadequacies."

"I wish I could think like that."

"You know what you need?"

"What?"

"More girl time. From now on, every Thursday we are going to that spa we got you a certificate for. We can bring Jamila along too. Make it a ritual."

"That's a great idea. Let's make it a date."

"Okay, honey. Now let me go find my loose-ass husband. I'll call you."

"Okay. Hey, Tricia, what was the girl's name?"

"Something like *Tera*."

"Hmm, that name sounds familiar." Donna began to think.

"Look, Jacob, I already told you a million times, I don't know this Tera you're talking about. Sorry, I can't help you locate her, but if I do by chance run into her, I will tell her to give you a call." Dominic knew what Jacob was up to and he wasn't falling for it.

"Good looking, man. Thanks for your help."

"Whatever," Dominic said.

Tricia walked in on them. "Hey, baby, you ready to go?"

"I'm ready. Good night, Dominic." He gave him dap.

Dominic kissed Tricia on the cheek and thanked her for coming.

"Lovely party, Dominic. We must do this again sometime." And the Evanses left the Joneses.

Dominic was left with the task of coming up with an excuse to sneak out to see Tera. He found Donna lying on the
sofa, apparently sleeping. *Problem solved.* She'd had too
much wine. He lifted her and carried her upstairs to their
bedroom, pulled off her clothes, and put her in bed.

Just as he was about to sneak out to see his girlfriend, his
wife woke up. "Hey, baby, how did I get upstairs?"

"I carried you up, honey. Go back to sleep."

"Where are you going?"

"I was going to sleep in the guestroom. You seem pretty
knocked out, and I didn't want to disturb you."

"You're being awful nice to me. Come to think of it,
things have been pretty good between us lately."

"When haven't things been good?"

"You know, with my mood and all. You've been extra
careful not to upset me. I appreciate that."

"Don't you know I would do anything for you?"

"Except make love to me."

"What do you mean? We make love all the time."

"Not lately. It's been months."

"Really? I guess it's this deal I've been working on with
my Asian client. I'm sorry, honey. I don't mean to neglect
you."

"Come here."

Dominic gave into Donna's advances and made love to
her. He figured he was doing her a favor, since it was her
birthday and all. But the entire time, he imagined he was
having wild, passionate sex with Tera.

Chapter 14

Tera was furious with Dominic for standing her up. She'd waited all night at Dawson's Place to see him and he never showed up. She was beside herself and wanted some answers. She didn't check herself once to come to the realization that she was his girlfriend, not his top priority. Tera was reacting like she was his only priority. And if Dom didn't know that, he soon would.

"Where the fuck were you?"

"Excuse me? I must have the wrong number." Dominic was a bit confused. He knew Tera would be upset, but cussing and carrying on was totally uncalled for.

"Dominic, don't play with me. Where were you?"

"Sweetheart, I do apologize, but on the real, don't ever curse at me like that. Those types of things will get you cut off in a heartbeat."

"I'm sorry, but I really wanted to see you the other night."

"I know, but things couldn't be helped."

"And you are just now calling me? It's been days since you called me back."

"I've been busy. You know, I'm a businessman and you know I have a family to look after. I can't just drop whatever I'm doing to see you."

"A family to look after? I know you weren't thinking about your family when your dick was in my mouth."

"Tera, I have to go now. Call me when that sexy, sophisticated, charming woman I met at the dinner party comes back. Because I don't know who the hell you are." Dominic hung up.

Tera couldn't understand why he was treating her like this. She called him for two days straight afterward and he didn't return any of her calls. She became so strung out on him that she had to see him.

The following week, after Dominic finished tidying up some business with a client, he left work early. He thought he would go to the gym and then try to catch up with his homeboy Seth. Since Donna was getting more into "serenity" and finding her inner spirit through meditation and Tera was acting a fool, his only option to release tension was a good workout and a nice long talk with his boy. He knew Seth would get his mind focused away from all the negativity he was experiencing lately.

As Dominic walked to his 7-series BMW, a very attractive young lady caught him off guard. "What are you doing here? You haven't returned my calls. I had to see you," Tera said.

"Well, now you see me. I have to go."

"Wait. I'm sorry for how I reacted. I've been going through

some personal things with my family. I know that is no excuse for my behavior, but I miss you."

"Have you washed out that yuck mouth?"

"Depends." Tera gave Dominic a sensuous grin.

"On?"

Tera French-kissed Dominic and grabbed his penis. She caressed it with tender loving care. After unzipping his dress pants, she knelt and began to show him what a naughty mouth she really had.

Dominic tried to ease up, fighting the thought of someone seeing them in the parking lot of his building. *I own this building, fuck it.*

Tera continued to stroke his ego and let him have his way with her as he grinded her and pounded her against his BMW.

After Dominic finished "parking-lot pimping" with Tera, he decided to still keep his engagement with his boy Seth, who lived about forty-five minutes away from Dominic's job. So he had time to listen to his John Legend CD and ponder over the events that just took place.

Although he enjoyed the excitement that Tera brought, he started to wonder if he could put up with her mood swings. Dominic had real commitments and priorities that kept his attention and needed his full devotion. Tera was not on that list. Frankly, none of his previous girlfriends were.

Dominic sighed at his next thought. *I might just have to let another one go. Damn, she seemed so right. I thought I could carry on like this with her until the end of time, but she is starting to act a little too clingy, needy and downright unappreciative.*

After all the gifts and getaways we have gone to in the last five months, she wants to act ungrateful. What has gotten into her?

He dreaded having that conversation with Tera. Unfortunately, if she kept up her behavior, he was going to have to cut her off as well. *Oh well, and another one.*

Chapter 15

Saturday morning was hot and humid at 100 degrees. Dominic promised Donna and Dawson they would spend a getaway at their cottage in Cape Cod. He needed to relax, and wanted to catch up with his girls. Since Donna's birthday, she had seemed more into herself than ever. She started really exercising, not just turning on a Billy Blanks VHS and bouncing around as she cooked dinner, but she and Dawson walked almost every day. She started eating salads instead of cheesecake from the Cheesecake Factory. She even joined an adult ballet class that she went to every Monday evening. Donna didn't think Dominic noticed, but he did. She was doing her own thing, and it seemed like almost a wake-up call for Dominic.

Dawson had cheerleading practice four times a week during summer break, so she was also too busy for her father.

Dominic felt his women slipping away from him, so he

wanted to take back control and make sure they were still in love with him.

The cottage was old but cozy. They invited their friends up there the first weekend and spent the second alone.

Dominic was able to work from the cottage to keep a watchful eye on his ever-growing business. The Joneses enjoyed fishing and scary bonfire stories. Dominic thought his teenage daughter was too old for that kind of stuff, but she really enjoyed it. After two weeks of vacation, it was time for the Jones family to come back to reality. Donna wanted to keep up with her routine, spending more "me time" and focusing on herself for once, and Dawson wanted to make sure her stay as co-captain for the varsity cheerleading squad wouldn't be tested.

As for Dominic, he was back to his unfaithful ways. After blowing Tera off for almost three weeks, he wanted to see how she would react. She was blowing up his voice mail on his cell phone every day, and not being able to meet up with him at his office was probably driving her insane. He decided to give her a call.

"Hey, baby girl, are you busy?"

"No, sweetheart. Why, are you trying to see me?" Tera asked innocently.

"Of course, you know I've been missing you."

"Why don't you come by after work, say around eight p.m.?"

"Sounds good. Your place or our spot?"

"My place. See you at eight."

"Until then. Kisses." Dominic made a puckered lip sound.

Tera hung up.

Dominic was in his glory. That's all it took. Just leave a ho strung out over the magic stick and it brings her back to reality. He thought things would finally get back on track with his girlfriend.

Later that night at Tera's Brookline condominium, Dominic arrived at eight p.m. sharp. Although he made love to Donna regularly while he was at the cottage, he yearned to have Tera do it to him the way he wanted it done. She was a serious no-holds-barred freak—Handcuffs, whips, Ben Wa balls, creams, and Kama Sutra positions. He loved that stuff and couldn't wait to get back in the saddle. He thought maybe he could even convince her to have a three-way with him and his secretary Monique, but wanted to play his Mack Daddy hand first.

Dominic rang the doorbell. No one answered for at least ten minutes.

Dominic grew impatient and began to knock on Tera's door. When he did, he noticed that it wasn't locked. A chill ran up his spine. Something wasn't right here. He could feel it.

As he entered Tera's apartment, the door swung closed. Dominic turned around quickly. "Why didn't you answer the door?"

"I wanted to surprise you." Tera hugged him and kissed him passionately.

"You miss me?"

"Of course, I did. Are you hungry?"

Dominic laughed. "Since when do you cook?"

Tera laughed with him. "I have cheese and crackers and some wine."

"I'll take a glass of wine."

The couple sat on Tera's suitor-financed leather loveseat and drank champagne.

Minutes later Dominic said, "You know, I wanted to talk to you about your attitude. It needs to change. You know your position, and if you want to keep seeing each other, then you better recognize. No more late phone calls, no more a million messages, and no more showing up at my office unannounced. Understand?"

"No."

"Excuse you?"

"I said no. Things are going to be different from now on. It's time you start recognizing my feelings and the meaning of this relationship. I want more."

"Sweetie, there is no more. You are on a budget just like the rest of my women. A penny here and a penny therrrrre." Dominic was beginning to slur his words. He wasn't much of a drinker, but he knew damn well one glass of wine, wasn't enough to get him tipsy. He felt out of body almost.

"From now on there will be no other women. I'm taking over," Tera said, with a devilish grin.

"You've lost your mind. I've got to go. Call me when you get some 'act right.'" Dominic rose from the loveseat but immediately fell to the floor unconscious.

Tera had slipped him a Micky. "Shaniece, it's time," she called.

Dominic woke up the next morning at eight, buck-naked in her condo. He cursed her out and couldn't believe she drugged him. He found his clothes and told her he never wanted to see her again.

Tera laughed at him and told him she wasn't ever going

to let him go and he might as well get used to spending more quality time with her.

A furious Dominic stormed out of her condo vowing to let her rot in hell before he ever saw her again.

It caused a serious blowback with his wife. She had called him several times, worried about him. Of course he lied and said he had a last-minute out-of-town meeting with one of his prestigious clients in D.C., and it was top secret, so he couldn't divulge any information until the project was finished. He thought that was a pretty good lie and was sure Donna bought it.

But a growing shadow of doubt was festering in Donna's mind, even through her meditation, exercising, or her change in mood that was starting to make her feel good about herself. She no longer would be so accepting of Dominic's loose behavior. She too wanted things to be different.

A week later Dominic received an anonymous manila envelope at his office. He hadn't spoken to Tera since waking up at her condo and was hesitant to open the mysterious envelope, afraid of its contents. But he manned up to it and reminded himself just who he was. *Dominic Jones, the wealthiest man in the city. Why should I dread an envelope?*

He should have stuck with his gut, because the contents inside were riveting. There were eight 8 x 10 photographs of him and Tera in their birthday suits getting their freak on. Or what appeared like they were getting their freak on. One of Tera giving Dominic some head, another of Tera riding him while he was tied to her bedpost, another one of her sitting on his face, another one of him hitting it from the back, another . . .

Dominic looked through all eight photographs until he came to the little vixen's note:

I just wanted you to see who loves you most and who can only do the things for you that YOU DREAM OF. But if you don't want others to see, I understand. We can keep it our secret, only if you can.

CALL ME
Smooches
Tera

Dominic was furious. None of his girlfriends ever pulled a stunt like this. He was starting to realize he wasn't dealing with an amateur. He reluctantly called his girlfriend to find out where she would like her remains to be desecrated.

"I got your mail, bitch, and I just would like to know what makes you think I would let you breathe another breath before I would let you blackmail me. Do you know who the fuck I am?"

"Dom, is that you? Hey, baby, did you get my love note?" Tera said cheerily.

That unnerved Dominic. *She must be crazy.* "What do you want?"

"What I've always wanted. You."

"Not going to happen."

"Dom, don't be silly. We have a great time together. We make each other happy. Just know from now on, there will be no more getting back to me when you feel like it. No more, fuck me, and then leave me. I need more."

"No can do, bitch. Find another sucka."

"I don't mean to hurt you, baby, but you left me no choice. Divorce your wife, marry me, and things will not get so ugly for you in the future, baby. Trust me, it's the best solution."

This bitch has lost her mind. "Eat a dick, Tera. You're real good at that. Don't ever call me again, you hear me. If you do, I won't be held responsible for my actions." Dominic hung up. *What the hell have I gotten myself into now?*

Chapter 16

Tera knew Dom would come around sooner or later. She didn't want to have to push him, but he left her no choice. She was tired of waiting around for him to love her the way she wanted. Somewhere in their relationship, she fell in love with Dominic and desired more from him. Being his girlfriend wasn't enough and she thought she deserved more. She knew he would resist in the beginning, but ultimately, he would realize that they were meant to be together. She had broken all the rules with Dominic. It was like her previous notion of getting what she wanted from men by using sex wasn't what she wanted with Dominic. She thought he was too good to just be used. She genuinely loved him and would do anything to keep him.

For the last couple of months, Tera was living to be with Dominic. She forgot to tell Shaniece about James. So this afternoon (they'd planned to meet at Friday's on Newbury Street) she was determined to come clean and tell Shaniece why James hadn't returned any of her calls.

"Tera, you know that was wrong what you did?" Shaniece took a sip from her margarita.

"What are you talking about?" *She couldn't already know. Did James tell her?*

"That stunt you pulled with Dominic, I thought you said you loved him?"

"I do love him and he loves me. He just needs to get his priorities straight. He should be with me, not some hippo housewife." Tera laughed, remembering the sight of Donna.

"Wasn't it you who always said you never wanted to be in the wife's shoes, being a girlfriend was too much fun?"

"That was because I never met someone like Dom. He is wonderful and just what I needed to make me realize being in love and committed to each other isn't a bad thing."

"How can you be sure Dom will only be faithful to you?"

"I'm not sure, but I know one thing. No one will ever love him the way I do and he knows that. So I think that, coupled with the supersonic sex we have, should be enough." Tera smiled.

"This is what I've been trying to explain to you all this time about how I feel about James."

"The love I have for Dom is entirely different from what you feel for James. He doesn't love you."

"Yes, he does. Well, at least I thought he did. He doesn't return my calls. It's been months since I've seen him."

"That's kind of what I wanted to talk to you about." Tera sipped her glass of water before she broke the bad news to her cousin.

"What's up?"

"James hasn't returned your calls, because I told him to stop seeing you."

"Excuse me?"

"Listen, I only did it to protect you. I know what kind of man James is. You are too good for him. And if you're really looking for love, James isn't the one for you. Plus, he wasn't giving you anything to stick around for. Trust me, I did you a favor."

"What did you do?" Shaniece was becoming more furious by the second.

"I blackmailed him with sex. I fucked him, told him if he ever wanted it like this again, he needed to stop seeing you. After weeks of dodging his advances, I told him I never wanted to see him again and, if he tried to hook back up with you, I'd tell his wife. Trust me, it was for the best. If he was so willing to stop seeing you because I wouldn't sleep with him anymore, then he definitely didn't give a shit about you. You see, I was only trying to help you."

Shaniece threw the rest of her margarita into Tera's face.

Tera gasped.

Shaniece stood up. "All these years I have been making excuse after excuse for you, blaming your parents abandoning you for the way you turned out. Everyone in our family warned me about you, how you don't give a shit about anyone but yourself. But I stood up for you, because I loved you and thought I understood you. But for you to do this to me, and to make it seem like it was all for me is the last straw. I don't ever want to hear from you again, you trifling, selfish bitch." Shaniece walked away from the table.

Tera chased her. "Wait, I'm sorry. I did it for you. You have to believe me."

"You did it for yourself. All you proved to me is what a

real whore you are and the lengths you will go to, to get your way."

"Shaniece, wait, you are all the family I have."

"I'm all the family you *had*. You are dead to me now." Shaniece snatched her arm away from Tera's grip and continued to walk away from her and out of her miserable life.

Later that day, trying to forget about Shaniece, Tera schemed to get Dom's home address and phone number. She called his secretary and pretended to be a teacher from Dawson's school. She told her the school had misplaced all of Dawson's emergency contact information because the school was vandalized over summer break and their student files had been stolen. Since they knew who her father was, they were able to contact him through his business.

Because she sounded very convincing, Monique gave her the information since Dominic was out of the office.

Tera was very pleased with her scam and even happier to find out where the Joneses lived.

Even though getting what she wanted from Monique brought some joy to her, she still felt empty. She hadn't heard from Dom or Shaniece in days. She was feeling hurt over her cousin's abandonment. Shaniece was the only person, other than Dom, that she really cared about. She was sick over their fight. She couldn't stop vomiting since that day and felt sick to her stomach. Tera wasn't going to be happy until Dom was completely in her life. She also would have to find a way to get her cousin back in her life.

But first things first, she had to get rid of Donna.

Chapter 17

Instead of their usual Saturday routine, Donna decided she wanted to go out to dinner with her family. After taking Dawson school shopping, the plan was for her husband to meet them at home. Donna's new regimen was making her feel more alive. And she was losing some weight. Down to a size twelve, she couldn't believe she could wear Seven jeans.

She and Dawson were getting along as well. She still nagged her about going to college, but lightened up a little, remembering she was a teenager too. Donna felt young again. Her Prozac stabilized her mood, but the meditation, exercising, dancing, and weekly trips to the spa with her girlfriends made her happier than years of therapy and medication combined. Donna was ready to start living. Now she just needed to get her marriage back on track.

Dominic came home later that evening with an unexpected surprise. He still wasn't sure what he was going to do about the Tera situation, but he knew she couldn't be avoided. He worried about the repercussions of their relationship.

For the first time in his life, Dominic didn't think he had control. *The nerve of this bitch, trying to force me to leave my wife. She isn't wrapped too tight. How could I not see this coming? Fuck. What am I going to do?*

Dominic agreed to meet his wife and daughter at their house. He spent his Saturday afternoon at the gym, then having a man-to-man about his Tera situation with Seth. But Seth didn't have any answers for him either. He got on Dominic's case about his cheating ways and how it would always come back to bite him in the ass at the very end.

Because of all the drama, he looked forward to a nice quiet evening with his family.

"Hey, baby. Are you ready to go?" Dominic kissed Donna on her cheek and snuggled her neck with his face.

"Yeah, we were ready an hour ago," Donna told him. "We said seven o'clock. It's going on eight. And you still smell like the gym, which means we have to wait even longer for you to get ready."

"Hey, what's with the attitude? I'm here now, and I'm starving, so let's eat." Dominic didn't know where his wife's attitude was coming from, but he didn't like it. He went up to his bedroom, showered and got dressed.

Half an hour later, he was ready to take his family to dinner at the Grille, a low-key restaurant outside downtown that served signature steaks that were grilled right at the table.

"Dominic, I forgot. This package came for you today. It was sent overnight mail." Donna handed him the manila envelope, similar to the one Tera sent him in his office.

Dominic trembled inside and feared what might be in the envelope.

"There's no return address and it's addressed to D. Jones,

so I assumed it was you, seeing how neither Dawson or I are expecting any important packages overnight."

"Let me see it, honey." Dominic pretended to examine the envelope. "Yes, these are the projections for that big overseas business deal I've been working on. I'm going to work on them this weekend."

"You? Work on a weekend? That's a first."

"Well, this deal is real important. It's a multi-million-dollar deal that could put us in the best financial position ever."

"I thought we were already in the best position, Daddy."

Dominic hugged his adoring daughter and ignored her question. The women in his life were all getting on his nerves. "Let me put this in my office. I will be back."

Dominic hurried to his office, ripped open the envelope, and dumped the contents on his desk. To his horror, it was the pornographic pictures Tera took of them. He was mortified because now he knew Tera had his address. He tucked the photos away in his desk and locked them. He was shitting bricks. He didn't know what Tera was going to do next.

After dinner, the Joneses were stuffed and worn out. Donna enjoyed the evening, but Dominic couldn't relax. He felt someone watching them, but didn't see Tera anywhere. He expected her to pop up at any moment and not only ruin his family, but their dinner as well. He wasn't prepared to let that happen. He was on edge.

He should have been, because Tera was watching the lovely Jones family from afar. She wanted to see if Donna got the pictures she sent her, but from the looks of it, she still seemed to adore her husband. She wanted to go over there and spoil Donna's dinner, but couldn't risk exposing their relationship without proof.

The sight of Dominic with his wife made Tera so sick that she threw up in the restroom several times. After the last trip to the bathroom, she almost panicked because when she came back to her table the Joneses were gone. She quickly paid for her dinner and ran to her car.

As the Joneses were driving off, Donna noticed that someone appeared to be following them. Every time they turned, the silver Mercedes CLK coupe would turn as well. She mentioned it to Dominic, but he ignored her. She didn't want to argue in front of Dawson, so she didn't pursue it. The car got closer and closer to the bumper of Donna's convertible and made her nervous.

"Who is that?"

Dominic shrugged. "Probably a drunk driver."

Donna wasn't convinced. She watched the car intently, becoming more and more afraid. "Maybe you're going too slow. Let them pass you."

Dominic continued to ignore his wife and concentrate on the road. He recognized the license plate "My Girl" and the car a mile away because *he* had bought it for Tera.

At the next stoplight, Tera pulled her car up to the driver's side and stared at Donna.

Donna recognized the woman but couldn't recall from where. "I think I've seen her before."

Dominic didn't want to look because he wasn't sure how he was going to handle the situation. He looked over at Tera anyway.

She stuck up her middle finger and said, "Fuck you, Dom," and peeled off and took a right at the next intersection.

A furious Donna said, "Who the hell was that?"

"How should I know?" Dominic shrugged his shoulders, trying to keep his cool.

"She said, *F* you, Dominic. Where do you know her from?"

"I don't know what you're talking about. She didn't say my name."

Lying again. Donna knew she wasn't crazy. Maybe her mood was unstable at times, but her hearing was just fine. She dropped it, but secretly made a mental note of the evening's fiasco with the mysterious woman.

Dawson noticed her parents weren't so happy after all.

And Dominic's fear began to turn to rage as he planned to deal with his scheming girlfriend once and for all.

Chapter 18

"Daddeeeee, telephone!"

Dominic paused for a moment. *Who could be calling at this hour?* "I got it, Dawson. Hang up."

A female vixen's voice came through the earpiece. "I need to see you."

Once Dominic recognized the voice, he whispered, "You know damn well that isn't possible! How the hell did you get this number?"

"I'll tell you when I see you. Meet me at our spot in one hour."

"An hour? Now I know you have lost your mind, Tera. You will be waiting forever because I'm not seeing you tonight."

"You sure are, Mr. 'Dick-me-down' Jones.'"

"Look, I told you I can't. We're in the middle of dinner."

"I don't really care. One hour, Dominic."

Donna yelled from the living room, "Dominic, we are having dinner. Who are you talking to?"

Dominic froze. "It's Monique from the office."

Tera gave out a vindictive laugh. "Tell your wife you will be having me for dinner tonight."

Dominic was caught up. Tera had his home number, his house address, and god knows what else. He had to do something about her immediately. "Okay, I'll meet you in one hour. Don't call here again."

"I won't have to, if you give me what I want."

"We'll talk later."

"Later, baby. I love you."

Dominic hung up. After last night's stunt he didn't know what Tera was capable of. Donna kept grilling him for information so much last night that he slept in the guestroom because he couldn't take it anymore. Donna was starting to ask too many good questions, something she'd never done before, and Dominic didn't like it. He needed to get his house back in order fast and that started with dealing with Tera.

After eating Sunday dinner quickly, Dominic had to come up with another lie to get out of the house. "I have to work at the office. I'll be back later tonight."

Donna questioned as she put the dinner dishes in the dishwasher. "I thought you said you were working from home this weekend?"

Dawson was off in her own world, talking to one of her schoolmates on the telephone.

"There are some things I forgot at the office. So I might as well finish my work there instead of coming back home."

"Dominic, we need to talk. You still haven't answered any of my questions about that woman."

"I've answered all the questions you've asked me, Donna. I've got to go."

"But, Dominic . . ."

He kissed his wife on the lips and then left.

Dominic may have made it out of the house, but he was still under serious scrutiny from his wife. In the past Donna suspected him of having affairs, but she'd never pursued her intuition because she didn't want to have to do something about it. For the first time in their marriage, she was ready to do something about it.

"Bitch!" Dominic stormed through Dawson's Place. "Where are you?"

"I've been waiting for you. I've missed you."

Dominic couldn't understand Tera's behavior. He lunged for her and grabbed her by the neck and slammed her against the wall they once had sex on, and then he slammed her to the floor.

Tera laughed through her pain as she tried to speak between her gasps for air. "I love you so much. Can't you see that?"

Dominic was in another zone. He looked into Tera's help-less hazel eyes and released his grip. "You're fucking crazy."

Tera tried to recover from her lover's near strangulation attempt. She sat on the bed in their exclusive love nest and stared at Dominic from across the room.

"How did it get like this?" Dominic asked, trying to find the same woman he enjoyed spending time with.

"I love you. I want it just to be us."

"That's not going to happen. I've told you that many times. Now, this has got to stop."

"What's your solution? You can't give me what I want."

"But I can give you what you want the most." Dominic took out his checkbook and wrote Tera a check for one hundred and fifty thousand dollars. He gave it to her and she was silent.

"I know what you want most. Money. It's the same with all of you women. You don't love me. You love what I can get you. You love the idea of a man like me. Take the money, baby. It was fun, but it's over."

Tera was still silent.

Dominic got up and kissed her on her cheek. "Take care of yourself, kid." He almost made it out of there, thinking he had put his problem to bed.

"You filthy, filthy son of a bitch. You think I'm some high-priced hooker or some kind of whore that you can just fuck me and leave? This isn't over. We will be together."

Dominic continued to walk out, ignoring his girlfriend's rage.

Tera jumped off the bed and rushed up to him. "Since you won't do it, I'm going to get rid of that bitch-wife of yours and let your precious Dawson know what a piece-of-shit father you really are."

Dominic spun around and smacked the life out of Tera. She landed across the room on the floor.

"If you think for one second I would let that happen, then you underestimate my power. I will kill you long before you get the chance to think of a way to destroy my family."

He walked up to Tera and stroked her face. "Cash the check, Tera. And stay the hell away from my family, or I'll see to it that this pretty little face isn't recognizable to ID your body." Dominic's words were as cold as ice. He stared

Tera down and gave her a look that meant he wasn't kidding. "No more, Tera, no more." Dominic slammed the door behind him.

Tera was shaking. It appeared that smack knocked some sense into her. *Would he really kill me?* Tera lay on the floor in a fetal position, crying and rocking herself to sleep, afraid to even move.

Dominic raced back home before Donna realized it was after one a.m. He couldn't believe how the tables had turned against him. He used to get so much pleasure from being able to sleep with Tera then going home to play his role as the perfect husband. It had never dawned on him that his unfaithful ways would finally catch up to him, that one day, he would lose control and suffer the consequences. He tried to break it off with Tera, but she wouldn't let go, wouldn't accept it. *Guess the loving I gave was too good,* he thought. *I didn't want things to come to this, but what else was I supposed to do?*

Under no circumstances was he willing to leave his family for any woman. He'd considered telling Donna, but that would've just added fuel to the already ignited flame. So Dominic was left with the only solution to his problem—Tera had to go.

Chapter 19

"Mr. Jones, there's a woman out here to see you. She says she's your girlfriend," Monique reported to Dominic over the office phone.

Dominic's throat became hoarse, shocked with fear. "Send her to my office and fix Mr. Tanaka some of that green tea." *Now what the hell?*

"Excuse me, Mr. Tanaka, I have an urgent matter to take care of. I will return momentarily." Dominic bowed his head, conforming to Asian custom.

Mr. Tanaka did the same.

Dominic flew past Monique's desk and into his office. He closed the door behind him and began his rampage. "You have lost your fucking mind! I told you it was over. How dare you show up here after I paid you one hundred and fifty thousand dollars to go the fuck away. And I know you cashed it, gold-digging bitch."

Tera looked as if Dominic's words of wrath meant nothing. She walked up to him and French-kissed him passionately.

Dominic pushed her away. "Are you insane?"

"Insanely in love with you. I know you said to stay away, but I know you didn't mean it. We belong together."

"That confirms it. You have lost it. How about you use that money to see a shrink." *She's a fucking headcase.*

"I don't need to see anyone but you. Don't you understand?"

"Look, I don't have time for this bullshit. I'm in a very important meeting. We are finished here for good, Tera. Now you saw your way in, so follow your footsteps and find your way out."

"Wait. I'm pregnant."

Dominic didn't flinch or show any emotion.

"I found out today. That's why I came over here like this. I know this changes everything now. See, we're meant to be together."

Dominic burst into laughter. "If I had a dime for every woman on the side who told me that, I swear I could quit my day job." He continued to laugh.

"I am. Look, here are my test results."

Dominic waved them away. "I don't care what those results say. My solution is getting rid of it. I want no part in that, even if I am the father. I have a family. I don't want another."

Tera broke out in tears. "You would just kill our baby?"

"Woman, please . . . Do you think this is the first time this has happened to me? I have sown so many wild oats in this city and others. What? You think you are special or the only girlfriend I've knocked up? The solution is always the same, either my way or no way. And you thought we were meant to be? The truth is I can have you replaced by tonight. Now stop your crying. You have your whole life ahead of you. Don't worry, I will take care of the abortion. I'll take care of everything. Just go."

Tera sobbed. "I wonder if your wife will think I am not so special when I tell her I'm carrying your child?"

"Bitch, try it. You won't live long enough to be saying anything."

Her confidence shattered, Tera became frightened. For the first time in years, she had no control of her situation and actually feared for her and her unborn child's life.

Dominic could smell her fear and made one last attempt to end their affair. "Tera, listen, what we had was good, but you ruined it with this let's-be-a-family shit. It's over. This is not what I bargained for. You are not that same sexy, sassy, independent bombshell I met at that benefit dinner. You have become something else, and for that I'm sorry. But, like I told you before, under no circumstances am I ever going to leave my family for you or any other woman. It's just not going to happen. Go. I will take care of everything."

Dominic kissed a tearful Tera on her forehead as he motioned her toward the door. She didn't put up a struggle, almost as if she was in a state of shock. "Wipe your face. Don't let anyone see you like this."

Tera took out her handkerchief and wiped her face, even though she felt so low that she could care less about her appearance.

Dominic walked her to the elevator and waited with her until the elevator doors opened. He put her on it and he looked at her with pity. *Poor young thing, she's got it bad for me. Oh well, and another one.* He turned around and headed toward the boardroom, but not before he smacked his secretary on her behind.

To Tera's surprise, Monique looked as if she enjoyed it. Tera's feelings of fear and worthlessness were replaced by rage right as the elevator doors closed.

Dominic bowed. "Sorry for the wait, Mr. Tanaka. I had a business matter that couldn't be helped. Now, as you can see from my projections, Jones Consultants can have your system up and running in less than forty-eight hours. Plus add new software to the main data frame, which will prevent any future bugs or hacking. At Jones Consultants we believe in customer satisfaction, and with our track record, we assure you that any further problems with your system will be eliminated with our software. It's—"

Dominic was cut off in mid-sentence by a fuming Tera, who barged into the boardroom with fire in her eyes. "You son of a bitch, why don't you tell your client how you are willing to kill our unborn child and turn around and fuck your secretary."

Mr. Tanaka's slanted eyes opened wider, and his face turned red.

Monique tried to stop Tera's ambush but was too late.

"Monique, call security."

"Oh, what's the matter, Dom? I'm sure your client would love to know how Jones Consultants spends its money for their girlfriends' abortions and shush money."

Dominic attempted to silence Tera by tackling her, but Mr. Tanaka jumped out of his seat, causing his chair to block Dominic's path. He then closed his briefcase and speed-walked out of the boardroom.

Dominic followed him. "Wait, Mr. Tanaka, I can explain. This woman is crazy. She has mental issues and has been stalking me for weeks."

Mr. Tanaka said nothing as he waited impatiently for the elevator.

"Please hear me out," Dominic pleaded.

As the elevator doors opened, security rushed onto the floor, and Mr. Tanaka hurried onto the elevator, pushing the *L* button repeatedly.

Security apprehended the vixen and escorted her out.

"Fucking bitch! You just blew a multi-million-dollar deal!"

"Oh, well, looks like you won't be able to afford that abortion. I'm glad I cashed that other check."

Dominic motioned to strike her, but Monique held him back. "Joseph, please, just take her," Monique begged.

Joseph obliged, and he and his partner hauled Tera off.

"You haven't seen the last of me, Dom," Tera yelled. "You just wait and see."

A minute later, the office was quiet, and Dominic was back to business. "Monique, see if you can get Mr. Tanaka on the phone with me. Hurry."

"I think you should cool it for now. Give him some breathing room and a chance to forget what he just witnessed. You can kiss his ass later."

"Would you just do as I asked? If I wanted your advice, damn it, I would ask for it."

"If you wanted my advice, you would've stopped whoring around, and shit like this would have never happened."

"Now is not the time. I'm in no mood."

"Whatever. Things sure would have been different if you and I stuck together."

"Yeah, right, sweetie. You wanted me all to yourself too. You are no different."

"I sure the hell did, but God gave me the good sense to

leave you alone. You ain't ever going to change. You're such a ho."

"Can you just mind your damn business and get me Tanaka?"

"Whatever, boss. I sure would like to see you pull this rabbit out of your ass." Monique giggled. "And if you do, even I will suck your dick."

"Well, get your kneepads ready, baby, because it's showtime."

Dominic closed his office door and sat at his desk. *It's a shame how things turned out*, he thought. Tera was so fine and ripe. He thought they could continue their affair forever, but she had to go "psycho bitch" on him. It was sad to see such a beautiful and intelligent woman crumble before his eyes. He would have given Tera anything. Except a divorce from his wife.

Monique knocked on his door and announced, "Mr. Tanaka on line one."

Dominic cleared his head and talked Mr. Tanaka into meeting him for dinner at PF Chang.

After his phone conversation, he summoned Monique into his office.

She shut the door and grabbed a throw pillow from Dominic's leather sofa. She dropped the pillow at his feet, knelt on it, unzipped his dress slacks, and went to work on "Houdini's magic stick."

Chapter 20

Dominic drove home feeling pretty good about himself. He had gotten rid of his Tera problem and managed to salvage the deal with Mr. Tanaka. Over dinner he'd discussed facts and figures and left his personal life out of their meeting, until Mr. Tanaka brought up the fiasco that took place in the boardroom.

"I can assure you that my personal matters will not affect the way I run my business. It never has."

Mr. Tanaka nodded.

"I admit, I had a fling with the woman, but that's it. As you can see she took our affair a lot more serious, and it's my fault that I let it get that far. I guess I just got caught up."

Mr. Tanaka sipped his tea but still said nothing.

Dominic thought Mr. Tanaka would surely decide to seek out another firm to handle his business matters and was surprised when he sealed the deal.

Dominic shook his hand. "You will not regret this. Jones Consultants is the best firm for your company."

* * *

He nodded. "I agree. In my country, we have a wife and concubines. But that isn't accepted here in America."

Dominic smiled. "Aye, I wish it only was."

"I too enjoy the company of other women besides my wife, so I'm quite familiar with your situation. Let me offer you some advice—When you enter a woman, know that you are entering her core and you must be both hard and slow with her in all aspects. Her body, soul, and mind are connected to that core."

Dominic didn't take Tanaka's advice lightly and hoped that his situation with Tera was resolved.

He reached in his suit pocket to turn his cell phone back on. He didn't want any interruptions during his meeting with Tanaka. The second his Nextel powered up, his message alert chimed. Before he could check his eight messages, Donna's cellular ID popped up on his incoming-call screen.

"Hey, baby."

"Where have you been? I have been trying to get a hold of you for the last three hours," Donna said frantically.

"I was in a meeting with Mr. Tanaka. Why? What's the matter?"

Yeah, right. Donna was getting sick of the lies. "Dawson has been in a car accident. We are at the General in the ER."

"Is she all right?"

The phone reception was getting bad; Dominic couldn't hear Donna. "What? Is she going to be okay?"

Donna's phone disconnected.

"Hello? Donna, are you there?"

Dominic pressed end and got off the first exit on I 93

South to turn around and get onto I 93 North. He was going ninety miles per hour, while unanswered questions sprawled in his head. *Oh no, not my baby, not my baby girl. Please let her be okay, please Lord. I will stop my philandering ways, if you please let her be okay. Please.* It was the first time in years Dominic sought a power higher than himself.

He parked his SUV in front of the hospital and jumped out of his vehicle.

"Wait, sir. You can't park there," a security guard explained.

"Then move it for me." Dominic threw the man his keys and rushed inside. He ran toward the Emergency Room sign, his heart pounding.

Once inside, he searched for Donna. No sign of her. He ran up to the front desk. "Excuse me, my daughter was in a car accident. Her name is Dawson Jones."

The receptionist took her time locating Dawson's name and finally stumbled upon it. "Here it is. Her mother is back there with her now. Are you Mr. Jones?"

"No, I'm the tooth fairy. Didn't you just hear me say I'm looking for my daughter?"

"Don't get smart. Press on the door. Your daughter is in bed four."

"Thank you." Dominic did as he was told and rushed to find bed four, hoping his daughter was alive when he reached her. He spotted the bed and pulled back the curtain. "Baby."

Donna was hovering over her daughter, who had a broken nose, busted lip, and a wrist splint on her right forearm.

"Daddy," Dawson cried.

Dominic hugged his frail daughter as his nerves slowly calmed down. "Are you okay? What happened?"

Donna looked at her daughter, who was thrilled to have

her knight in shining armor there with her. "Dominic, I told you she would be all right. She'll need a wrist cast." Donna tried to conceal her disgust.

"The phone cut off. I didn't hear that. I'm just glad she's okay. What happened?"

"Dawson, your father and I are going to step out for a minute. We'll be right back."

"But he just got here. Can't he stay a little longer?"

"Yeah, we can talk on the way home, Donna. I want to spend time with my baby."

"Dominic, I said I need to speak to you now. This can't wait."

Dawson began to sob, regressing to a five-year-old needing her father's attention. "It hurts so much, Daddy."

"What hurts, baby? Tell Daddy where."

Dawson pointed to her right wrist.

"Where is the doctor? What are they giving her for pain?"

"Dawson, cut it out. You know you're trying my patience. If I have to cut up in here, I will, and you're going to need more than some pain medication, you hear me?"

Dawson was sobbing heavily.

"What is the matter with you? Don't you see our daughter is hurt?"

"What I see is Dawson crying wolf and you falling for it time and time again. Now we are going outside right now to talk. And Dawson knows why. We need to discuss what happened in private."

"I'm sorry, Daddy, but she ran me off the road."

"Who did?"

"Damn it, Dominic, your daughter stole my car and went joyriding with her friends."

"What?"

"Daddy, I'm sorry."

"How did she get your car? Where were you?"

"Fuck you!"

Who in the hell does this woman think she is talking to? Dominic grabbed Donna by the arm and pulled her outside. "We'll be back, baby."

Down the hall of the ER, the Joneses got into it. Still grabbing her arm, Dominic proceeded to scold his wife, "Don't you ever disrespect me in front of my child like that again. Woman, you know I would—"

"Save it, Dominic." Donna snatched her arm from his grip. "You should be ashamed of yourself, coming in here all concerned, when you have been whoring around like a cheap prostitute."

"What did you call me?"

"You heard me. I am sick of your lies and your bullshit. You have the audacity to ask me where was I when this happened. Where the fuck were you when our daughter was being run off the road by one of your trifling bitches?"

"I don't know what you're talking about, but you better lower your voice. Dawson isn't the only one who bumped her head. Are you sure you weren't in that accident?"

"Just admit it, Dominic. How long? How long have you been having affairs?"

"For the last time, woman, I don't know what you are talking about. How did Dawson get a hold of your keys?"

"Today is Thursday."

"And?"

"Of course, you wouldn't know. Every Thursday is spa day for me. My girlfriends and I take a limo and go to the spa to get pampered, then we get our hair done, and then we catch a movie and dinner. I have only been doing this for the past two months. But I guess you never noticed because you were too busy fucking every cunt in sight."

"Woman, if you don't stop cursing at me . . . So you left your car at home, and Dawson decided to go joyriding?"

"This probably isn't the first time she's done it. Who knows how long she has been doing this. She knows my schedule like clockwork. More than I can say for you. I just thank God she dropped off her friends before this happened. But mark my words, Dominic, I am going to hunt down that no-good hussy of yours and run her over my damn self."

"Donna, please." Dominic giggled inside at the thought. True, this shouldn't be taken lightly. But the thought of Donna taking charge and handling her business with Tera turned him on a little.

"Who is she?"

"I don't know what you're talking about. There is no one."

"Bullshit."

"Let me have to tell you to watch your mouth again."

"You can sit there and protect her, after she tried to kill your daughter?"

"Her who? Speak English, woman."

"Dawson gave the police the same description of the car and the woman driving that I told you was following us from The Grille last week."

"There was no one following us."

"You ignored me then, but you will not ignore me now. Your little girlfriend was stalking us last week, and this week she tried to kill my daughter."

124

Dominic sighed. "What?"

"She wasn't trying to run Dawson off the rode. She was trying to run *me* off the road. She thought I was driving."

"Woman, you are really—"

"Shut up, Dominic. That's right. We drove my car last week to the restaurant. She pulled up to my side of the car. She turned off when she saw you."

Dominic tried not to let his worry show. "Donna, again, I don't know what you are talking about. No one is after you or us. Dawson is okay. She gave the police the description of the car and the woman. They'll handle it. Let's just go home and take care of our daughter."

Donna, deep in thought, agreed with Dominic and decided to put her interrogation on hold. She knew Dominic was seeing someone else and would never admit it. What she didn't know and what scared her was, if this woman was capable of harming her, how far would she really go? Donna's animal instincts began to kick it. *That bitch doesn't know who she's dealing with. No one fucks with my family.*

Dominic and Donna returned to their injured daughter. The doctor released her and wrote her a prescription for pain.

On the way home, they stopped to have Dawson's prescription filled. There was no conversation, just silence thereafter. However, their thoughts were in unison. Both Donna and Dominic were thinking, *She's going to pay for this.*

Chapter 21

The next couple of days in the Jones home were chaotic. Dominic stayed home from work Friday to take care of his daughter, and to put Donna's mind to rest about Tera.

Make no mistake, Dominic planned to seek revenge on Tera for the stunt she pulled. She wasn't going to get away with almost killing his only child. His first idea was to burn down her condo in Brookline with her in it. His second was to haul her off to the Sahara Desert and bury her alive. He wanted Tera to suffer by any means.

Dominic couldn't believe what a fatal attraction that woman turned out to be. Tera was the perfect girlfriend until she caught the let's-get-married bug. *She should know she isn't the marrying kind. If she had stuck with the program, I wouldn't be sitting here contemplating murder.* He should have known when Jacob was so eager for them to meet. Funny, in trying to screw his rival, he screwed himself.

Not wanting to go through this again, Dominic considered doing background checks on his next girlfriend. Once

Tera was out of the picture for good, he could focus on that, but for now his main problem was finding an excuse to get out of the house so he could deal with her.

The phone rang three times. Donna answered, but it was another hang up. She knew it was her. But what she couldn't understand was how she got their home number. All day she avoided Dominic because the sight of him made her sick. All these years she'd sensed he was dipping out on her, but it never mattered more until one of his girlfriends tried to harm her family. Although she didn't have any proof there were tell-tale signs, like the scent of unfamiliar perfume on his clothes, the late meetings, the out-of-the-blue business trips, and his overall lack of interest in sex. She thought she could live with the possibility that he had affairs, as long as he didn't bring home any diseases and continued to take care of their family.

"That was another crank call from your little girlfriend," Donna said, disgusted.

"Not this again. For the last time, baby, I don't have a girlfriend."

"And you can just sit there and let her do this to our family. She nearly killed our only child, Dominic."

"Dawson is fine. The police will catch up with that reckless woman." *But not before I do.*

Donna let out a cynical laugh. "I know you're not serious. What's her name? If you won't handle the bitch, I will."

"Enough of this already." Dominic was growing tired of her questions. If she kept it up, Tera wouldn't be the only woman he'd have to get rid of.

Their dispute continued throughout the day, evening, and night. Dominic had the nerve to try to make love to Donna, but she locked him out of their bedroom, and he was forced to sleep in the guest room.

By Saturday, the arguing had gotten worse. It got to the point where Dawson had to turn up the volume on her TV to drown out her parents' heated discussion.

By evening, Dominic was fed up with Donna and had just about all he could take. "I'm going out," he said to Donna while she was preparing their dinner.

"The hell you are. Not with your psycho-bitch girlfriend running loose and you're not doing a damn thing about it."

Dominic backhanded her across the face. "I told you to stop cursing at me in my house."

Shocked, Donna held her face, which was burning hot, and remained silent.

"I'll be back later."

"I hope you never come back."

Dominic turned around and grabbed Donna by the throat. "Now you listen to me and you listen good. I've had enough of your lip. I don't want to hear no more about this shit. Even if I was seeing another woman, what are you going to do about it? Divorce me? Yeah, right. You couldn't find a judge in this town to give you squat. I'm not spending my hard-earned money on alimony. I'm the king around here, and it's high time you start recognizing that."

Realizing Donna was about to lose consciousness he let go of her neck, and she fell to the floor, gasping for air.

"I don't know what the hell has gotten into you. Maybe too many trips to the spa with your girlfriends—which I pay for, I might add—have gassed your head up. You would never leave me because you wouldn't survive. And if you think you would take my only child away from me, then you are really crazy." Dominic grabbed his car keys.

Donna could hardly speak. "Dominic."

"What?"

"How could you treat me like this?"

"You brought this on yourself."

Donna began to cry.

"Oh, come on, baby. Why do you do this to me? I'm trying to make it right. You just have to trust me."

"Trust you? I don't even know who you are anymore," Donna said, sobbing loudly.

"Baby, you know who I am. I'm devoted to you and Dawson. Can't you see that?"

"No, not when you hurt me like this."

"Look, I'm sorry, but you went too far. We can talk about this when I get home."

"Where are you going?"

"There you go with the questions again. In fifteen years of marriage, I never had to explain where I'm going. I'm not about to start now."

Still sobbing, Donna got up off the kitchen floor. "I can't do this anymore."

"You are not divorcing me. I have worked too hard to keep this family together."

"You can't keep threatening me like this, running off to your whores whenever you feel like it."

"Donna, I'm warning you, please don't make me hit you again."

She broke out in tears again. "You don't love me. You don't love us."

"I don't have time for this. I have to go."

"Go then. Be with your tramp who tried to kill our daughter."

Dominic moved closer to Donna to slap her silly.

"Why are you making Daddy so mad, Mommy?"

Dominic turned around. "Baby, it's okay. Go back upstairs."

"No, Daddy. Mommy, what did you say? You're always saying something to make him leave."

"Dawson, if you don't get your little ass up them stairs and into your room, you will regret it for the rest of your life." Donna sniffled. "This is adult business."

"Don't cuss at her, woman. Dawson, go to your room!"

"But, Daddy, I want to go with you."

"I'm not going to repeat myself. You can't go with me."

Dawson stormed off, giving her mother an angry I-hate-you look.

Donna cried again, angry and hurt that her daughter blamed her for their unhappiness.

"See what you've done? I'm through arguing with you, Donna. I'll see you when I get back."

"And when will that be?"

"When I get back."

When Dominic left out the garage door, Donna threw the bowl of fresh broccoli at the door with all her might and broke down crying again.

The phone rang, and Donna answered. "Hello." There was no answer, but she could hear someone breathing on the other end.

"I know it's you, you tramp bitch! You are going to regret the day you ever fucked with my family. If you ever come near us again, I will hunt you down, kill you, and feed you to the pigs."

A woman's voice laughed through the receiver.

Donna hung up. She swore on everything she loved, her husband's girlfriend would pay dearly.

Chapter 22

Torturing Donna was a joy for Tera. She wanted her to know that soon she would be out of the picture for good and Dominic would belong to her. She figured Donna would get the hint and leave Dominic or else suffer her. She couldn't understand what Dominic saw in his pathetic wife, an ugly duckling compared to her. A fat, unattractive housewife who didn't have enough sense to leave.

Tera knew she and Dominic belonged together and that the baby would be a new beginning for them. She was hoping for a boy because she knew Dominic longed to have a son. Donna's inability to at least do that for him was reason enough for Dominic to desert her. What kind of wife can't even give her husband a son? In Tera's book, Donna had played her last hand, and she was ready to take her place as Dominic's wife.

Honestly, Tera couldn't understand how she'd allowed herself to fall so hard for him. She would have never guessed in a million years that she'd find someone who made her want to get married and raise a family. All her rules had changed. Now she was following her heart.

As Tera dreamed on about her life with Dominic, the phone rang. "Hello."

"You trifling bitch, now I hear you're pregnant with James's baby."

"Shaniece?"

"Yeah, it's me. How could you?"

"I don't know what gossip you heard at the salon, but I'm pregnant with Dom's baby."

"Yeah, right. You and I both know whose baby that is. How could you be so selfish?"

"Look, I know you're upset, but I don't have time for this."

"I thought you would always look out for me. I loved you like a sister."

"Shaniece, I was only trying to show you what kind of man James was. I never meant to hurt you."

"Liar! You have always been that self-serving bitch. You don't deserve to live, let alone be a mother."

"I see, you still don't get it. Whatever you think doesn't matter anyway. Dom and I are going to get married and raise our baby."

"Ha-ha-ha! Believe that shit if you want to, but that man knows you ain't nothing but a gold-digging tramp."

"Think what you want, but it's true. I'm hanging up my days of being a professional girlfriend to be a wife and a mother. Dominic will take care of me now."

"It's too late for you, bitch. You are going to get what you deserve, just wait and see." Shaniece hung up.

Tera didn't let her cousin's animosity get to her. She continued with her thoughts that Dom would come around soon and finally give her what she wanted.

Dominic raced back home in the moonlight. He had no other choice but to get rid of Tera for good. There was no other option. She'd crossed the line. He'd warned her about coming near his family. He only wished he had handled her better before things led to this. She wouldn't go away even after he paid her. Now she was talking marriage and becoming a family, not to mention the nutty stunt she'd pulled in front of his million-dollar client, Mr. Tanaka. It was clear, the bitch had to go. *She's lucky I didn't kill her then. No one's going to miss her anyway.*

For a moment he considered leaving his philandering days behind him to focus more on his family. *After all, how much ass can one man have?* He laughed to himself. *As much as he can have.*

Despite his wandering penis, Dominic knew this was a sign. Because of his selfishness, his daughter was almost killed, and his wife was losing her mind, cussing and disrespecting him, showing her ass. Before this, she never behaved this way, especially in front of their daughter.

If Tera could snap after six months of his loving, Donna was sure to be on the brink of insanity after fifteen years. It was time to get his house back in order. Dominic made a decision to stop sleeping with other women, and to be faithful to his wife and devoted to their family. It was long overdue. Plus, he couldn't go through another mess, if he decided to find another girlfriend. It was becoming way too dangerous.

* * *

Beaten and shot in the head, Tera lay in her own pool of blood. As her life began to fade, she had only one thought in her mind. Her unborn child. She would've done anything to save her child's life.

Up until the time she met Dominic, fell in love, and got pregnant, she felt so empty inside. In all her twenty-four years, she had never felt so alive. Now that was being taken away from her. She knew she deserved to drown in her own blood, but not her baby. Not the only love she would ever know. All Tera knew was how to be with another woman's husband. Being unattached, uncommitted, and unloved was all she could identify with, and now that love was finally getting around to her door, it was too late.

Tera struggled to breathe. Then darkness crept in and took her and her unborn child.

Chapter 23

The Jones's doorbell rang late Sunday afternoon. Detective Mark Anderton had some questions that needed to be answered immediately. Even though his co-worker had warned him, Mark went with his gut feeling, deciding that Dominic Jones had a lot of explaining to do.

Donna came to the door, puzzled, because she wasn't expecting anyone. When she opened it and Mark showed her his police badge, her heart raced.

"Mrs. Jones, I presume? I'm Detective Anderton with the Brookline Police Department. Is your husband at home?"

Donna cleared her throat. "What is this in regards to?"

"A murder investigation."

"Murder?" Donna's heart began to palpitate faster. "What? Who? Excuse me, did you say murder? Oh my God." Donna couldn't get her words right. "Why do you need to speak to my husband about a murder?"

"I was hoping he could answer a few questions."

"I think he might need his attorney present then if he is—"

Mark cut off Donna. "I just have a few questions for him about the deceased. If he needs an attorney present for that, then I will have to ask him to come down to the station."

Dominic approached the door after catching part of his wife's and the detective's conversation. "I'm Dominic Jones. What can I do for you?"

Finally. "As I told your wife, I'm a homicide detective, and I have a few questions I'd like to ask you in regards to a murder."

"Please come in." Dominic was as cool as ever.

They sat in the living room, and Dominic hurried Donna away to get them something to drink.

"So what's this about?"

"Do you know a Tera Larou, Mr. Jones?"

"Tera? Sorry that name doesn't sound familiar."

"Really? Well, she was murdered sometime last night or early this morning."

"Murdered? That's awful. Why do you think I knew her?"

"Your number was in her phone book, and your home number was the last one she called before she was murdered."

Dominic was still calm. "Really? Isn't that some kind of coincidence?"

"Not really. It seems the victim knew you, along with some others. Look, I'm not going to beat around the bush, and I will say this since your wife is out of the room. It appears Ms. Larou had quite a few, as she called it, 'suitors' listed in her phone book. It doesn't take a genius to figure out the victim was quite the busy girl, if you know what I mean."

"No, actually, I don't."

"So you're telling me that you weren't having an affair with the victim?"

Dominic pretended to be appalled. "How dare you? I told you I didn't even know the woman. The entire city knows who I am and what I do. It doesn't surprise me that Ms. Larou had my number in her phone book. If not all, half the women in this city would love to be with me. But I'm happily married."

Mark wasn't buying it. "Really. Then Ms. Larou had her eye on you. Is that what you're trying to tell me?"

"It wouldn't be the first. I'm very well known here. You should know that, Detective. I've sponsored many campaigns and charity funds for the police department and the mayor."

"I'm aware of who you are, Mr. Jones."

"Then you are aware of who I know?"

"That doesn't mean I can't question you about a murder."

"Fair enough. But really, if you have any other questions, I'm afraid I would like to have my attorney present, seeing how you've made your own conclusions about me and Ms. Larou."

"I haven't drawn any conclusions yet, but I do know you're not telling the truth."

"Are you calling me a liar in my own home?"

"If the shoe fits." Mark couldn't stand Dominic or people like him who thought, just because they had money, they could do what they pleased.

"I'm going to have to ask you to leave." Dominic stood up and gestured for Mark to follow him to the door.

Donna walked in, still confused. "What's going on?"

"Nothing. The detective was just leaving."

"Oh, by the way, Mr. Jones, where were you last night between the hours of ten p.m. and two a.m.?"

"I was home."

Mark looked to Donna to confirm that, and she nodded her head.

"Okay then. Nice to meet you, Mrs. Jones." Mark left his business card on the coffee table. "If you think of anything else about the victim, Tera Larou, please don't hesitate to call."

"Nice to meet you too," Donna said. *Where do I know that name?*

Dominic literally pushed Mark out of the door. "I doubt we'll need to call you, but if you have any other questions, contact my attorney."

"Oh don't worry, Mr. Jones. If I have any more questions, you will be the first to know." Mark smiled and left the Jones's residence. He could sense Dominic was hiding something and wouldn't rest until he got to the bottom of it.

Later that evening after dinner, Dominic said he needed to go out.

Donna knew from the other night not to question him and wanted to avoid another fight in front of Dawson, but she had burning suspicions now. She followed him out to the foyer. "Dominic, we need to talk."

"Not now, Donna, I have to meet with Luke. I think this detective might be a problem."

"Why? Where'd you go last night?"

Dominic grabbed her by her forearms and pulled her close to him. "Listen to me, Donna. You can never let anyone know I went out last night. If there is one thing I learned from my father is to never rely on the police to help you. All they ever want is to see a wealthy black man like myself behind bars. It doesn't matter how high you climb, there will always be someone waiting to bring you down. Do you understand?"

Donna nodded.

"I know things haven't been great between us, but know that I love you and Dawson more than anything in this world and I'd die before I let anyone hurt you."

Donna became frightened. "What did you do?"

Dominic smiled and let go of his wife's arms. He held her in a bear hug. "Nothing that you wouldn't have done, sweetheart. Can I count on you?"

"Yes."

"Do you love me?"

"Of course, I do."

"Then trust me. Everything's going to be fine." He released Donna and kissed her gently on her lips. "Remember what I said. I love *you*, Donna."

Dominic left his wife with those words and sought to clean up his dirty laundry.

Donna cleaned up the kitchen and was ready to go to bed. It was ten o'clock and she was exhausted from the weekend's drama. She had had all she could take of Dominic's unfaithful ways, but a part of her wanted to work out their marriage and get past the awful things that happened that weekend. She started to go upstairs to her bedroom until she heard the television playing in the den, where Dawson was watching the news.

"Baby, it's time to go to bed. You need your rest. We have

to go to the doctor's office tomorrow, so they can put the cast on. Do you hear me talking?"

Engrossed in the late-night report about a brutally murdered woman, Dawson ignored her.

"Late last night or sometime this morning, the victim, Tera Larou, twenty-four, was murdered inside her condo here at Brookline Condominium."

A photograph of Tera appeared on the TV screen.

"The victim suffered one gunshot wound to the head. She was also beaten with an unknown object. The police currently don't have any leads but are questioning those who might have known the victim. If you have any information, please contact the Brookline Police Department. This is Beverly Smith reporting live at the scene for Channel Seven News. Back to you, Bob."

Donna's heart started to palpitate again, and she began to tremble. Dawson, you need to go to bed, honey."

Donna used the remote to turn off the TV. She was in her own thoughts, but she noticed her daughter was also trembling. "What's the matter?"

"Nothing. Leave me alone," Dawson shouted, and ran up to her room in tears.

Donna didn't know what had gotten into her daughter and couldn't focus on that right now. She had finally put the pieces of the puzzle together. *Tera . . . that was her name . . . the same woman in the bathroom, the same woman who tried to kill me, the same woman Dominic was having an affair with. Could she also be the same woman Tricia was telling me about? I need answers.*

She picked up the telephone and called Tricia's house.

"Hello," Tricia answered.

"It's me. I need to talk to you as soon as possible."

"I know. It's about her, isn't it?"

"When can you meet me?"

"Tomorrow. Your house. Around one."

"Dawson has a doctor's appointment in the morning. We should be back by then. I'll call you."

"Okay. See you then."

"Thanks, Tricia."

Donna began to get a headache. She drank four glasses of white zinfandel to calm her nerves. Then she finally drifted off to sleep.

Chapter 24

Luke Bennet had been Dominic's trusty attorney for several years. Whenever Dominic was in a legal bind, Luke always came through. Dominic trusted him with his life, literally, plenty of times in the past, and he knew if there was someone to get him out of a jam, it was Luke.

Luke could argue his way out of anything, and with his Morris Chestnut smile and Billy Dee Williams coolness, he was as handsome as he was talented. Fair skinned, with a caramel complexion, and gray-blue eyes, he stood six feet tall and had a muscular build. His hair was always cut low, with deep waves, and his mustache trimmed to perfection. His looks could get him anything he wanted, and he was as persuasive as a snake charmer. In fact, Luke was the typical pretty boy and a perfect ally for Dominic.

Although it was a Sunday night, Luke agreed to meet Dominic at his downtown office. The security guard let Dominic into the closed building and signed him in at the front desk. As the elevator to Luke's office was taking its slow time, Dominic tried to get last night's events out of his head. He didn't mean for this to happen, but Tera posed a bigger threat alive. She just wouldn't let go. *What else was I supposed to do?*

After arriving in Luke's office, Dominic thanked him for meeting him so late and shook hands with a firm grip.

"No problem. It sounds like you really needed to see me. What can I do for you?"

"A woman I was seeing was murdered, and the police already suspect me. I've worked too hard to let everything and everyone I hold dear be destroyed. How can I make this go away? Can you talk to the mayor?"

Luke and Mayor Mennings had been friends since college. In fact Luke was the one who introduced Dominic to the mayor, and they both thoroughly supported him and in return received special favors, legal and illegal. Every politician has his price, and Dominic always used that to his advantage.

"I'll do my best, but a murder case is going to be hard to just make go away, man. Have a seat and tell me what happened."

Dominic went on to tell Luke about his affair with Tera and how she turned psycho on him. He told him about the incident with Dawson and then about the meeting with the detective.

"This hot-shit Detective Anderton seems to want to make this personal. He gave me the impression that he wasn't going away easily."

"Okay. Maybe I can see if we can get him off your back,

but for now what I need you to do is to get rid of anything, or anyone for that matter, who can tie you to the victim. You said you were seeing this girl. Did you buy her things?"

"Yes, but I paid for them all in cash and put everything in her name . . . like the Mercedes."

"Good. Did you ever meet any of her friends or family members?"

"Come on, Luke, you know me better than that. Of course not. I only saw her."

"How about people at your office?"

"My secretary, but she will never say anything. Of course, there was that scuffle with my security officers. They hauled her out of my office last week."

"So she was stalking you?"

"Yeah." Dominic recalled something. "Oh shit!"

"What?"

"I wrote her a business check for one hundred and fifty thousand dollars."

"Okay. We can say it was fraud or some oversight. Especially if she was stalking you and tried to kill your daughter. That explains the calls, her having your number, etcetera."

"There is one other thing."

"What? I need to know everything, Dominic."

"She took some pictures of us and tried to blackmail me with them."

"Where are the pictures?"

"Locked in my desk at home and at the office."

"Destroy them."

"I'm sure she had the negatives."

"Even so, photos can be admissible in court. Let me take care of that, if it goes there."

"Then I guess that is it."

"Good. If you forgot to mention anything else, call me."

"Oh yeah, she said she was pregnant with my baby, but she could have been lying. Shit! From the sounds of her address book, it could have been some other sucker's baby."

"Exactly. We'll worry about that if it pops up. For now, if that detective continues to snoop around you or your family, I want you to call me. Maybe we can get him taken off the case for harassment or something."

"I don't want him anywhere near the case. He has it in for me, I can tell. He's got to go."

"I'll see what I can do. Just keep playing cat and mouse with him. Don't admit to anything, and make sure no one in your family talks to him. You have an alibi for last night?"

"Yeah, I told him I was at home."

"That will have to hold for now. You're a prominent member of this community, Dominic. Anyone who thinks he can bring you down has got a hell of a fight coming his way."

"My thoughts exactly. That's why I wanted to see you as soon as possible."

"I'm glad you did. Don't worry. I'll take care of everything."

"I know you will. I'm paying you enough."

"And you know I'm going to bill you for this, right?"

"What else is new?"

The two men shook hands again and said good night to each other.

Dominic was feeling more at ease because he knew he had the right people on his side. *Who does this detective think he is, trying to bring me down? I own this city.* Dominic kept thinking positive thoughts in his head and tried to push out images of Tera moaning in agony as he beat her with a wine bottle.

Chapter 25

Donna's nerves were getting worse by the minute. She got up early, cleaned her bathroom, meditated, took her twenty milligrams of Prozac, cooked breakfast, and straightened up the living room and den all before nine a.m.

Dawson had a hard time getting out of bed, bargaining for an extra minute every time her mother popped into her room like the Energizer Bunny. Finally Dawson gave in and got up and got dressed for her ten a.m. appointment with the orthopedic doctor.

Donna was still on edge and couldn't stand still in the waiting room at the doctor's office, pacing back and forth so much. The secretary assured her that her daughter would be fine.

Realizing she was making a spectacle of herself, Donna went down to the lobby and got a cup of herbal tea. Then she called Tricia to confirm their afternoon meeting and raced back up the steps to see if Dawson was ready yet.

The drive home from the orthopedist was silent. Usually Donna would nag Dawson about something, but today she was at a loss for words.

Dawson wasn't up for much conversation either. She was troubled about something but wouldn't open up to her mother.

Donna was so busy worrying that she didn't notice her daughter's mood had changed. Finally she broke the ice and told her of her lunch plans for the day. Then she added, "So if you want you can invite a friend over or something. I know not being able to go to cheerleading practice is killing you, but it will be there in six weeks, once the cast is taken off. And all your pom-pom buddies can sign your cast in the meanwhile."

"That is so fourth grade. I'm not a child, you know, Mother."

"I know, but you will always be my baby, no matter what."

"Can we just not talk right now? I'm tired, and I just want to go back to bed."

"Fine. But if you need anything, I'm here." Donna put her nagging on hold for the day. Like Dawson, she wasn't in the mood.

Donna and Tricia sat out on the patio for lunch. Donna had made chicken Caesar salad with low-fat Caesar dressing and wheat rolls. She also made fresh lemonade, and placed a bottle of white zinfandel on the patio table as well. She knew she was going to need a drink sooner or later.

It was a sunny, breezy fall day. The leaves on the trees weren't ready to change color and fall, but the cool breeze blew over the trees very calmly.

Donna poured her friend some lemonade and fixed her a

plate of lettuce and chicken. She didn't want to be the first to say it, but couldn't help herself. She sighed. "So you heard it on the news as well?"

Tricia took a mouthful of her lunch and swallowed hard. "I did."

"I can't believe this."

"You didn't know her, did you?"

"It's a long story, but she was also seeing Dominic."

Tricia almost choked on her lemonade. "What?"

Nodding, Donna broke out in tears.

Tricia handed her a napkin. "Don't waste your tears on her or your husband. You have to pull yourself together. Did the police question Dominic?"

"A detective was here yesterday. What about Jacob?"

"A detective Mark something came by early this morning before he left for work. He was trying to be secretive with me, saying the detective was just covering leads and so forth, like I'm some kind of idiot. But I know why he was questioning him."

"Jacob still has no idea you knew about the woman?"

"Not a clue. And I want to keep it that way. But I don't think the detective had anything on him, because he didn't stay long and he didn't ask me any questions when my cheating-ass husband summoned me back into the room. As if I wasn't eavesdropping on their entire conversation anyway." Tricia smirked.

Donna tried to relax. "What a coincidence! The same woman was seeing both of our husbands?"

"Too much of a coincidence. It wouldn't surprise me if Dominic met her at that benefit dinner that night. You know he and Jacob can't stand each other and have always been in competition with one another. So it doesn't surprise me one bit that they were sleeping with the same woman. Bunch of hoes, they are."

"So what's next?" Donna asked. "Is this detective going to keep questioning us until he finds out something?"

"He can't invent things to find, sweetie. He's just covering all his bases. And from what I heard, that hussy is giving him a lot to cover."

"What do you mean?"

"I mean the woman was some kind of professional. She had two hundred and fifty-four men's telephone numbers in her little black book. She called them suitors. So I'm guessing she did this for a living. Slept with married men, and then got all she could out of them, before she blew the whistle on them."

Donna poured herself a glass of wine. "Are you kidding me?"

"I'm not. Shit! I think I'm going into that business. Sleep with married men, get their money, and move on to the next. It sure beats sitting around trying to keep a so-called husband, trying to hold your family together when your husband is out screwing just about everyone." Tricia's eyes were getting misty.

Donna understood where her friend was coming from and wanted to cry some more, but didn't. She held Tricia's hand. "I can't believe I'm saying this, but we are strong, sweetie, and that is why we stick with our unfaithful husbands. We are the backbone, and we try very hard to not let our family fall apart."

Tricia sobbed. "I know, I know. It just hurts, damn it. It hurts so much." Tears streamed down her face. "And for what? To be humiliated? To be looked at as the poor naïve wife who can't live without her husband, so she chooses to ignore the fact that he is having an affair?"

Donna never saw her friend like this. Usually it was Tricia holding her hand as she cried a river on her shoulder. "I don't know what to tell you. I guess I've dealt with Dominic's shit for so long I really haven't dealt with it, you know. I've been preoccupied with my own demons and fighting depression that I couldn't handle, dealing with the kind of man I married. A cheater. A low-down rotten pig."

Tricia looked at her friend, surprised at her last comment. Then they looked at each other and laughed.

"I can't believe I just called him a pig." Donna giggled some more.

They both silenced their amusement and came back to reality.

"What are you going to do, Tricia?"

"I don't know, but I think instead of going on like this, waiting for another one of Jacob's girlfriends or ex-girlfriends to pop up dead, I'm going to have to really confront him about his unfaithful ways."

"I think it's time."

"It's long overdue, Donna."

Donna smiled at her friend, understanding what she meant. "It's time," she whispered, and the two got up and hugged each other under the fading sunlight.

Chapter 26

M ark was eager to get the final forensic report and autopsy for Tera Larou's murder case. "What do you have for me, Riley?" he asked.

Riley walked in with his morning Dunkin' Donut's coffee and a jelly doughnut. "The autopsy is back. Nothing much more than we already suspected. The bullet was lodged in the victim's frontal skull, causing her death. There were several fractures to her skull from a blunt object causing some sub-cranial bleeding. There was some bruising on the victim's body, her back, and arms, possibly from a struggle." Riley continued to summarize the report until he stopped at the next paragraph. "Oh shit!"

"What? Spit it out, Riley."

"Autopsy also reveals the victim was twelve weeks pregnant."

"Well, there it is—motive."

"Whose motive though? She was seeing two hundred and fifty-four men."

"I've interviewed them all, and there is only one who had the most motive and the most to lose if his dirty secret ever came out."

"Who?"

"Dominic Jones. It's him. I know it. I just need more proof."

"Here we go again. Didn't the chief tell you to lay off unless you had some hard evidence?"

"Yeah . . . well, the chief isn't the most objective in this. He's probably on Mr. Jones's payroll as well."

"You better not let him hear you say that."

"I don't care. A woman, a future mother, is brutally murdered and no one gives a shit but me."

"I'm not saying that, Mark, but you are taking this case way to personally. You're not being very objective."

"Whatever. Let me see the rest of that report."

Riley handed it to him and left Mark alone with his "baby." He sensed Mark had a serious "hard-on" for Dominic and didn't want to be anywhere near the fallout once the chief got wind of it.

Mark was the first and only African-American detective at his precinct in Brookline, so he definitely had something to prove. For years he'd been agonizing over taking the exam to become a detective, doubting he would ever make it.

His co-workers made stereotypical judgments about his life. They had no idea that Mark grew up in Jamaica Plain, and that his mother moved to West Roxbury when he was in the tenth grade. He graduated with honors from West Roxbury High School and attended Northeastern University to study pre-law.

During the last year of his undergrad study, his fiancée Krista was murdered, and that changed his life forever. Mark decided not to attend law school and joined the Boston Police Department to find her murderer. To this day, the case remained unsolved. Determined to bring her murderer and every other scumbag to justice, Mark fought for the city every day like he was fighting for Krista.

Eventually he made lead detective. Now many of the other candidates who once dismissed him, feared and respected him. There was still heavy animosity and racism at the precinct, but Mark just laughed and dared anyone to challenge him.

He worked seventeen hours a day putting the pieces together that would lead to Dominic's arrest, whose smug attitude made Mark work even harder to bring him to justice.

After going over the forensic reports and other evidence, Mark realized Dominic might not be the only suspect. Donna and Jacob were also possibilities. Donna's motive was pure rage and heartache from her husband's betrayal. And Jacob was the second-to-last suitor and possibly the father of her child. Mark would need a blood sample from both Dominic and Jacob to rule out paternity of Tera's unborn child. He didn't want Jacob or Donna, though, he wanted Dominic. So he needed to eliminate them from the picture.

Mark met Jacob at his office after he agreed to answer more questions without his attorney present. Jacob felt he didn't have anything to hide, especially since Tricia had kicked him out of their house after he refused to go to marriage counseling. Jacob still refused to confess his involvement with Tera to her, even though he knew Tricia was aware of the truth. He figured deniability was his friend, and if he never admitted it, Tricia would have to let it go. He was wrong.

Fed up with her husband, Tricia wasn't ready to let it go. If he didn't start putting their marriage first and admitting his faults, he would soon find that separation was a prelude to divorce and years of alimony.

Mark entered Jacob's office and smiled as he gave him a handshake. "Thanks for meeting with me again, Mr. Evans. I have a few more questions I need to ask you."

"No problem. What's up?"

"Why did you give Tera Larou one hundred thousand dollars?"

Jacob shrugged. "I didn't."

"Are you denying that a check for one hundred thousand dollars was made out to Ms. Larou?" Mark placed a copy of the cleared check that he kept in his pocket on Jacob's desk.

Jacob examined it. "Like I said, I didn't write the check. My wife did." He pointed to his wife's signature.

Mark smiled. *He's trying to be cute with me.* "Let me level with you, Mr. Evans. I know you are the owner of Evans Steele, and I know you were seeing Ms. Larou. And I know you are, quote unquote, happily married to your wife, Patricia Evans, and you have a son, Jacob Evans Jr., correct?"

"That's right. I don't see where you're going with this."

"I also know that if it came out that you possibly fathered a child by the deceased and thus became a suspect in her murder, it would ruin your business, your marriage, and your family."

Jacob was silent. He couldn't believe what he was hearing.

"Now, I know your wife signed the check to Ms. Larou. I can read, too. It's a prerequisite, you know, for the job and all. But what I don't know is why your wife would pay your ex-girlfriend with your money without you knowing about it. You see what I'm saying?"

Jacob tried to relax. "It's a long story. But I didn't father any baby with her. We were finished the night of the benefit dinner in March."

"Would you take a blood test to prove you're not the father?"

"Absolutely."

"So what about the money?"

"She wanted me to pay to help her start a business. I refused. So the night of the benefit dinner she showed up and my wife caught me with her. She pretended she was a rep for a college fund or something. Before I knew it, Tricia bought it and wrote her a check for one hundred thousand dollars for a scholarship fund. I didn't say anything because of the circumstances, but after that I never saw her again. In fact, I introduced her to Dominic Jones."

"I see. So she humiliated you and blackmailed you out of one hundred thousand dollars and you introduced her to your friend. Why?"

"It's no secret that Dominic and I are public friends because of our wives, but we despise each other. I figured introducing them would get her off my back and give him a taste of his own medicine."

"So you knew what kind of woman Tera was, and you wanted her to do what she did to you to Dominic."

"Exactly. And, who knows, maybe they would end up happily ever after."

"Why do you despise Dominic so much?"

"Because he's a phony. He grew his business from his father's drug money. He doesn't deserve any of the clout he receives in this town. He's nothing but a hood, a street punk. Do you know who his father was?"

"No. Who?"

"Kaleel Jones, aka The Dona. He was the most notorious drug-dealing gangsta this city has ever seen. His gang was vicious and responsible for most of the murders in this city in the late eighties. If he wasn't murdered nearly twenty years ago, I don't think this city would have survived his warpath."

As Jacob rambled on, Mark reminisced to that time when The Dona was the most feared and respected soldier in the game. He didn't know him, but he'd heard rumors about his shootouts and the millions he was making in the drug trade. Every inner-city kid wanted to be down with him, and those that didn't, wanted to see him fall. Mark never was into that life. He'd had his priorities with school, and he was in love with his lifelong girlfriend, Krista.

After she was murdered, the police never could find her killer, but word on the street was she was at the wrong place at the wrong time and got caught in some crossfire between two gangs. Even after Mark joined the force, he still couldn't get any witness to testify who was involved in the shootout. But one thing Mark did learn was that it was The Dona's gang who was warring with other local gangs over territory and drugs. Although it might not have been The Dona himself who was responsible for Krista's murder, Mark still hated him and was very happy when he was gunned down all those many years ago.

Jacob finished his history lesson with Mark and felt a little more at ease, knowing Mark didn't really have anything on him. He was even more pleased to know that Dominic was also a suspect, if not the primary suspect. It didn't surprise him. He knew Dominic was capable of murdering Tera. The apple doesn't fall far from the tree, and in Dominic's case, Jacob knew he was as ruthless as his father.

"One more question, Mr. Evans. Do you know for sure if Ms. Larou was seeing Dominic Jones?"

"I'm quite sure they were seeing each other because she told me."

"Who? The victim? When? I thought you said you hadn't spoken to her."

"I know, but after she scammed me out of my money, I called her, trying to reconcile, but she told me she was seeing Dominic Jones and didn't have time for me."

"Did that upset you?"

"Not really. I've never had a problem replacing my last girlfriend with a new one, so I wished her the best."

"Really? After she conned your wife out of your money and was seeing your enemy, you wished her the best? Come on, Mr. Evans, give me a break."

"Well, maybe it didn't come out exactly like that, but I was glad she was out of my life and out of my pocket, and even happier to know that Dominic would have to suffer her."

"I see. You're good friends with Mrs. Jones, aren't you?"

"My wife and her have been close for years, and I love Donna like she was family. That's why I tolerate her husband. Dominic doesn't deserve a woman like Donna."

"Did Donna know about the affair?"

"I don't think so. Why? You can't possibly think Donna had something to do with Tera's murder. She wouldn't hurt a fly."

"I'm just covering all my bases."

"Not Donna. She is too sweet a person."

"I see. Well, thanks for your time, Mr. Evans. We'll be in touch if I have any further questions."

"All right then."

Both men shook hands, and Mark saw his way out of Jacob's office.

Jacob was relieved, but hoped that the detective didn't pursue Donna. True, if she did know, who knows what a woman scorned would do? But he hoped, for Donna's sake, she didn't have anything to do with Tera's murder.

Mark on the other hand had his own agenda. Dominic Jones was the son of the man responsible for his fiancée's murder. If he couldn't have his revenge on The Dona, he would definitely make sure his only kin suffered the consequences.

Chapter 27

Donna slammed the newspaper in front of Dominic at the breakfast table when she read the headline.

Dominic sipped his orange juice and began to read the paper.

POLICE GET LEAD ON MURDER VICTIM'S KILLER

Last week, Tera Larou was found murdered in her Brookline condo early Sunday morning. After a thorough investigation by Brookline police, they believe the victim might have known her assailant. Police found evidence that the victim made a living as a "professional girlfriend," blackmailing some of the most prominent men in the city. The victim kept a little black book with more than two hundred telephone numbers of suitors. Police believe one of her suitors was involved with her murder. Detective Mark Anderton stated, "We will not rest until Ms. Larou's killer is found."

"Dawson, can you excuse your mother and I for a second? We need to talk." Dominic folded up the newspaper and smiled at his daughter.

"Whatever." Dawson left the kitchen and went upstairs to her room.

Dominic didn't like his daughter being short with him, but he allowed it because of the guilt he felt about Tera running her off the road. The article in the newspaper pissed him off, but he didn't want to let that on to his ever-worrying wife. He had to maintain order.

"Donna, don't worry. I told you everything is going to be fine. They just have to cover all their bases."

"Your number was in that black book, Dominic. You were seeing that woman."

"This again. Like I told the police, I didn't know the woman. She probably had me on her list as her next victim or something. That doesn't mean I was seeing her."

"When are you going to admit it? When it's too late? You're not trying to protect us, you are trying to protect yourself."

"I'm going to be late for work. I don't want to talk about this anymore."

"Dominic, wait. I've been thinking we should see a marriage counselor."

Marriage counselor? I don't know what gets into this woman's mind. Dominic got up from the table and went to his office to get ready for work.

Donna tried not to weep at the kitchen table, but she felt hopeless. Her husband still wouldn't come to terms with his involvement with Tera and continued to lie to her. *Lord, please give me a sign. I don't know what to do.*

* * *

Mark was still hot on the case. The evidence was pointing to Dominic, not just because he was the last one she was seeing, but because of the photographs of the two he'd found, the yet-to-be-cashed check for one hundred fifty thousand dollars made out to Tera from Dominic, and most of all because of the coroner's report that the victim was twelve weeks pregnant. He figured the victim was blackmailing Dominic, and once he'd found out she was pregnant, he decided to get rid of her permanently before his dirty little secret was exposed. Mark had it all figured out. He just needed more proof.

His chief was riding him hard about this case already, making it abundantly clear that he wanted everything done by the book, that gut feeling alone wasn't going to be enough to pursue Dominic. He wanted day-by-day reports on the case, and all evidence that pointed to Dominic run by him first.

Mark suspected that Dominic had something to do with his chief's watchful eye and personal interest in this case. That made Mark despise Dominic even more and work harder to get something solid on him. Mark couldn't see that he was taking this case personally, and that drive clouded his objectivity with hate for Dominic.

The next person on Mark's list to question was Tera's estranged cousin, Shaniece. He'd spent so much time trying to track down all of Tera's suitors that he barely had enough time to interview her family. Shaniece invited Mark over to her one-bedroom apartment in Dorchester to talk about her cousin.

Mark rang the doorbell. When Shaniece came to the door, he was almost knocked of his feet. He thought she was beautiful and had the most innocent smile. Dressed in a pair of Levi's jeans and a white knitted scoop neck top, her flip-flops showed her French manicured toenails. She had a short hair cut, like Halle Berry, and huge dimples that complemented her smile. Her eyes were hazel like Tera's, but almond-shaped.

He almost forgot why he was there. "Hello, my name is Mark Anderton. I'm a homicide detective." He was trying to get his words right. "You must be Shaniece. I mean Ms. Turner. Or is it Mrs.?"

"It's Ms. Turner, but you can call me Shaniece. Do you mind if I call you Mark?"

"No, not at all." Mark was at a loss for words again. He hadn't been this attracted to anyone since his fiancée.

After a long awkward silence, Shaniece asked, "Aren't you going to come in?"

Mark nodded. Then he tripped over the doorstep on his way in.

"Are you okay? I'm sorry about that. Sometimes these doorsteps can be tricky."

"I'm fine." *Clumsy bonehead. Get your shit together, man.*

"Would you like something to drink?"

"Um . . . a glass of water would be fine."

Shaniece disappeared into the kitchen. Mark looked around her apartment. It was neat and clean. He looked over her pictures on the mantel and saw a couple of Shaniece and Tera together, one when they were kids, another as teenagers when they were all dressed up, and another of them hugging each other on the beach.

Shaniece came out of the kitchen with a glass of water for Mark and one for herself.

"I'm sorry for your loss."

"Thank you. I would have contacted the police sooner, but I've been busy making funeral arrangements."

"Are your cousin's parents around?"

"No. They abandoned her when she was ten."

"That's sad. You two must have been close."

"Yeah, we were like sisters. I was all she had, and now she is gone," Shaniece said, tearing up.

Mark handed her a tissue from the coffee table.

"Thank you. It's just hard, you know. No one in our family got along with Tera. They basically acted like she didn't exist."

"That must have been hard for her. Did anyone wish her harm?"

"No. They just didn't want anything to do with her."

"That's kind of harsh, seeing how her own parents deserted her."

"I guess that's why she turned out the way she did."

"What do you mean?"

"It's no secret. I've seen the newspaper. My cousin made a living out of other people's misery. Mostly her boyfriend's wife's misery."

"That's what I'm here to ask you about. I understand if you don't want to go into it, though. I can come back another time."

"No, it's okay. I'd rather get this over with."

"Do you know who Tera was last dating?"

"Dominic Jones. She was in love with him and wanted him to leave his wife and marry her."

"Do you know if that was going to happen?"

"Tera made it seem that way. She claimed he was leaving his wife and that they were going to be a family."

"She was carrying his child?"

"That's what she said. She was so happy. She even said she was giving up her days of being a girlfriend to be a wife and mother to Dom's children."

"Dom?"

"That's what she called him. They dated for about five or six months. He bought her all kinds of expensive jewelry, clothes. They went on trips together. He even bought her a Mercedes."

"Do you know anything about this check for one hundred fifty thousand dollars he gave her?"

"No, she didn't mention anything like that to me."

"Do you know if Dominic ever threatened her?"

"I'm not sure, but I know he was pretty upset with her when she took those pictures of the two of them."

"Why did she do that?"

"I don't know. Tera could be hurtful and mean sometimes. She said she didn't mean to push him, but he needed to understand that they belonged together."

"That sounds strange."

"Yeah. Well, my cousin did some strange things."

"You were the last person to speak to your cousin. What did she say?"

"Just that she and Dominic were going to be a family. She sounded very happy. She was in love." Shaniece began to sob heavily.

"Okay, I'm not going to take up any more of your time. If you think of anything else, don't hesitate to call me." Mark wrote his home number on the back of his card. "You can call me day or night."

"Thanks. I appreciate that."

"And thanks for the glass of water." Mark smiled. He didn't want to leave and hoped Shaniece would call him. He knew it was unprofessional of him to leave his home number, but he really wanted to see her again. "Don't worry, Shaniece, I'm going to find your cousin's killer. You have my word."

Shaniece smiled and gave Mark a hug. "Thank you."

Mark wanted to kiss her, but decided to settle for the hug instead.

Chapter 28

Donna pressed the keyless entry button to her convertible. She'd just finished coming from the hair salon and was running late for her appointment with her psychologist, to whom she was making regular visits ever since Tera's murder. She was feeling so alone and hurt by it all. Dominic had betrayed her in so many ways that taking her antidepressants weren't enough to get her through the day.

All she ever wanted was to find love, get married, have children, and to be a dancer and choreographer. But marrying a habitual adulterer robbed her of ever having any more children, and the last time she was on stage dancing was when she was in college. And now that her husband's girlfriend was dead, that should have made Donna happy. After all, it wasn't like she saw any good in Tera still being around. Tera was tearing her family apart.

But Tera's death didn't sadden Donna one bit. Her life was what saddened her. It was all too much to bear. She wanted to escape this life. She wasn't contemplating suicide, but she desperately wanted the pain to stop.

As she opened the door to her car, she heard someone yelling her name.

"Mrs. Jones, I need to talk to you for a minute."

It was Detective Anderton. He was practically running to get her attention.

Donna wasn't in the mood for his interrogation. She ignored him and got in her car.

Mark stopped her from pulling off by standing in front of her car.

Donna rolled down the window. "Look, I don't think it's a good idea to be talking to you without my attorney present."

"Mrs. Jones, I assure you answering my questions shouldn't incriminate you . . . unless you have something to hide."

An awkward silence took over for several seconds as Donna seemed to have zoned out.

"Mrs. Jones, you knew about the affair, didn't you?"

Donna still wasn't answering.

"Look, I know that must have hurt you so much that you—"

Donna's attention came back to Mark. "So much that what? I could have killed her?"

Mark looked at Donna oddly. "Did you?"

"Of course, I didn't. But am I glad she's gone? You bet your ass I am."

"She tried to harm your daughter, didn't she?"

Donna was silent.

"I read the police report. Tera and her car fits the description your daughter gave to the police when she was in a car accident a couple of weeks ago."

"Leave my daughter out of this. That woman thought she was running me off the road, but Dawson was driving my car."

"This same car you're in now, right?"

"Look, I'm late to my appointment. I have to go. If you have any questions, you can relate them to my attorney."

"Wait. One more question, Mrs. Jones. Did you know the victim was pregnant?"

Donna gave Mark a death look. She didn't know Tera was pregnant and was mortified. *That fucking bastard. How could he?* Donna was in her zone again. Her heart was feeling heavier, all the weight of her marriage strangling her. She almost couldn't breathe.

From her look, Mark knew he'd just opened a big sore. "Are you all right, Mrs. Jones?"

Donna regained control over her heart. "I'm fine. Just leave us alone. Haven't we suffered enough?" She didn't give Mark a chance to answer and pulled off, with no concern whether she ran over his feet or not, leaving him with the closet of secrets he'd just let out.

She's no murderer, but her husband definitely is a son of a bitch.

Weeks later, Mark still didn't have enough evidence to charge Dominic with Tera's murder. (His chief warned him that it was all circumstantial.) Plus, he didn't have a weapon to tie to Dominic either. He questioned Dominic's secretary and his security officers, and more of Tera's family members and friends. He even tracked down the hotels Dominic and Tera stayed at when they took trips together.

One eyewitness even claimed seeing a silver car pull away from Tera's condo around the time of the murder, but it wasn't enough to convince his chief that Dominic had something to do with Tera's murder, or get permission for a warrant to search Dominic's house. Mark hit a dead-end and felt disgusted with himself. He could picture Dominic's devilish grin and wanted to rid the world of it. He wanted more than anything to have Dominic brought to his knees.

Mark felt even worse when he thought about Shaniece. He'd promised her he would find her cousin's killer. She would call him once a week to see if he had any updates, then they'd have a short conversation and that was enough for Mark. Just once, he would've liked to tell her that he got him. He enjoyed talking to her and wanted to see more of her, but first he had to get Dominic.

After another long day chasing leads, Mark was ready to call it a day. His desk phone rang. "Hello, this is Detective Anderton."

A woman's voice came through the phone. "Hello."

"Yes, can I help you?"

"I shouldn't even be calling."

"Who is this?"

"I have some information about that dead girl."

"Tera Larou?"

"Yes, that's her."

Mark listened intently as the caller claimed to have seen

Dominic coming out of Tera's apartment minutes after the time of the murder.

Finally . . . someone who can shed some light on this case. More importantly, give me the ammunition I need to arrest Dominic.

Chapter 29

Dominic and Donna got ready for the Black Business-men's Gala. He was nominated for the third time and was sure he was going to win. He had been in a very good mood since Luke told him the police still didn't have anything concrete on him. Dominic was happy he had connections to counter that hot-shit detective's leads. He knew no one in the city would stand against him. The police had nothing, and all he needed to do was enjoy his night and put the past behind him.

He was trying to make good on his promise to himself, to be a better husband and father. He wanted to be faithful, but Donna was making it hard. She kept nagging him about Tera, the murder, and about going to a marriage counselor. They hadn't made love since Tera's murder, and even longer before that. Dominic couldn't remember the last time he felt his wife's skin rubbed against his. Every other night, he was sleeping in the guestroom because Donna had locked him out of their bedroom. He was getting sick of it, and wanted to find someone to fulfill his needs, but he'd made a promise and was trying to stick to it.

He just wished Donna would return to being the loving, understanding wife he'd married. He knew she was upset about his betrayal and, even more, angry that he wouldn't admit it. But he believed deniability would save their marriage. It had gotten him out of every jam he could think of. Dominic just wanted his wife back. He just wanted things to be like they used to be when both the women in his life, Donna and Dawson, adored him and trusted him. But he knew it would be a long time before that happened. And for the first time in his life, he was willing to wait on it.

The gala was filled with all the prominent men and women in the city. The mayor was a special guest, and Jacob's wife Tricia was the MC for the night (her father had founded the association.) Everyone was dressed in black evening gowns and tuxedos. The hotel ballroom was decorated with black and white balloons and silver banners. Each table had a clear slender vase and white lilies as the centerpiece.

They served stuffed mushrooms and scallops wrapped in bacon, along with cheese and crackers as the appetizers, garden salads, the choice of filet mignon or stuffed lobster tails as the main course and a chocolate truffle cake for dessert.

Dominic was having a magnificent time. Donna played her part as his wife and pretended to enjoy boring conversations with politicians and businessman. She found comfort in talking with Tricia, though, but only for a short while, since Tricia's MC duties kept her busy.

Donna didn't enjoy the life she once did with Dominic. She thought it was all a lie and couldn't stand herself for allowing it to go on this long. Her Prozac and meditation kept her from sinking deep into depression, but she hadn't exercised or attended dance class in weeks. She tried to keep up her routine with her friends at the spa, but Tricia was always canceling and Donna didn't feel in the mood to go. Donna really missed herself and wanted things to change.

Tricia called everyone's attention as she announced this year's winner of the Black Businessman of the Year award. She announced the nominees first. Then the drumroll sounded as she announced Dominic Jones as the victor. The audience clapped.

Suddenly everything appeared to be in slow motion for Donna, who had four or five glasses of champagne, the audience's applause and voices seeming muffled, the room spinning. She sat down to compose herself, but became fixated on the policemen rushing the stage after Dominic. It all seemed unreal. Then she saw Detective Anderton reading Dominic his rights, as he and the other policemen hauled Dominic off the stage and out of the building. Donna tried to come back, but instead she fainted.

Chapter 30

The next day, everyone heard about what happened at the gala. It was all over the television and in the news-papers:

> "Dominic Jones of Jones IT Consultants was arrested last night for the murder of Tera Larou."
> "Dominic Jones is the main suspect in connection with the murder of Tera Larou."
> "Dominic Jones has been arrested for brutally murdering his girlfriend and unborn child."

It was the Jones's worse nightmare. The police searched their residence for evidence, but only found the porno-graphic pictures Tera had taken. No murder weapon. They searched and seized Dominic's clothing for bloodstains. They impounded all of their cars, except Donna's, because it was in the shop at the time of the murder. They still didn't find any evidence linking Tera's murder to Dominic.

Everyone from Dominic's grandmother to his secretary was calling the house. It got so bad that Donna had to turn off the ringer. Dawson didn't go to school that day. She stayed in her room and cried all day. The news reporters were camped outside the Jones's residence like bloodhounds.

Donna was on her fifth glass of wine for the day. She didn't take her Prozac or meditate. She wore her black evening gown from the night before. She didn't cook, clean, or bathe all day.

It wasn't until nightfall that the reporters finally left their lawn and the neighbors finally decided to go back inside their homes.

Jamila tried to call Donna all day, but with no answer she made a visit to her home.

Donna pulled herself together to look out the window to make sure it wasn't a nosy reporter or neighbor. She was happy to see her friend. She opened the door, and they hugged. "I'm so happy to see you." Donna cried. "I thought everyone deserted us." She continued to cry.

"I would never do that, my dear friend." Jamila didn't let go of her weakened friend. She ran her a bath and scrubbed her back, as Donna cried.

Jamila straightened up the house and made Donna and Dawson something to eat. Dawson didn't want to come out of her room, so Jamila took a tray of food up to her. "You know you can't stay in here forever, my dear."

"I know, Auntie Jamila."

"Your mom is going to need you."

"I know." Dawson began to cry. Her perfect world was crashing down.

Jamila let Dawson be alone, so she could tend to her friend.

"You have to eat, honey. You will get through this. Dominic will be fine."

"It's not him I'm worried about."

"Then who?"

"I'm worried about Dawson. I'm worried about this family. All I've tried to hold together has been destroyed."

"It's not your fault."

"Isn't it? If I would have stood my ground and left Dominic for the cheating husband that he is, my family wouldn't be going through this."

"Honey, you only did what you thought was best. That isn't a crime. If you left Dominic now, no one would blame you."

"I can't leave him now. Not when he needs us the most."

"I know, sweetie. You will do what's best for you and Dawson. You always have."

"Have I?"

"Yes, you have. You are a lot stronger than you know. I don't think I could have survived all the things you have, all the things you deal with every day. You'll be all right."

"I just feel so humiliated."

"Forget about what these people are saying. Your real friends are with you every step of the way."

"Dominic has a hearing or arraignment or something tomorrow."

"Say no more. I'm going with you. My clothes are in my car."

Donna hugged her friend again. She felt so lucky to have her.

* * *

The next morning at Dominic's hearing, the judge heard arguments from both sides. The DA presented evidence to indict Dominic of murder, and Luke countered by saying there wasn't enough concrete evidence to charge Dominic, and wanted the case dismissed. After careful consideration, the judge ruled in favor of the prosecutor.

The DA wanted Dominic held without bail because he posed a flight risk. Luke objected, stating that his family and business were both there and he had no reason to flee. The judge agreed with the prosecutor and held Dominic without bail. He set November 1st as the date for Dominic's indictment.

Dominic looked confused. He had worked with the prosecutor and the same judge on many projects in the past, donating heavily to their charity funds. He couldn't believe they hung him out to dry. He was beyond angry; he was on fire. He looked to Luke. "You said this would all go away. You have to do something for me, man. I can't go to prison."

"Don't worry, I'm on it."

"Not from what I can see. They're tearing me apart and you're letting them."

"It's not me, it's not them. The media is all over this. They think you are some kind of vicious baby-killer. We have to be careful. The powers that be are keeping a watchful eye. I'm on it, though."

"The powers that be? So I'm just suppose to be made an example of? I'm the fucking powers that be, nigger. You better fix this, so help me God, pretty boy."

Dominic was baffled at what just happened. He couldn't believe he had come this far and still was seen as some thug

179

or menace to society. Where were all his supporters? Where were all the beggars that were in his pockets? The mayor, the city councilmen, the commissioner, the chief were the people he'd paid good money to keep him out of messes like this. Where were all his friends that kissed his ass every chance they got?

Doesn't matter how much money or power you have, you will always be treated as a nigger. Cowards! He looked around the courtroom and he only saw the media and his family. He winked at Dawson and blew a kiss to Donna. "I'll be home soon, baby, don't worry. Daddy will be home soon."

The court officers hauled a furious Dominic away in handcuffs, and the reporters rushed out of the courtroom to get their stories to print first.

Donna was devastated but didn't want to cry in front of Dawson. Her daughter was doing enough crying for the both of them. Donna was still. She was looking for a sign, and she almost missed it.

Chapter 31

Dominic was indicted in November, and jury selection was due to begin soon. The news called him an animal for brutally killing his mistress and unborn child, allegedly. Anti-abortionists and other citizens who'd befriended him earlier marched outside the courtroom at his indictment. Donna's socially elite friends deserted her, and she was no longer invited to special events or asked to help raise money for charities. The once beloved and admired Jones family was outcast and despised by society. The opinionated couldn't understand why Donna stayed with her husband. Through all this turmoil, Donna couldn't understand either. The only ones who stuck by her and showed their support were her church and her two best friends, Tricia and Jamila.

Dominic's grandmother called almost every day. She was so worried about her grandson and prayed he would get through this.

Despite his wife's disapproval, Seth visited his best friend in jail and checked on Donna and Dawson from time to time.

Dominic appreciated the support he did receive and vowed that once he got out of this mess he wouldn't forget those who stood against him.

Meanwhile, Jones IT Consultants was taking a nosedive in stocks and business, as many companies pulled out and hired other IT consultants to fix their computer systems. Mr. Tanaka even pulled out his million-dollar account that Dominic had worked so hard to acquire. Even though, Jones's employees were more than capable of continuing to use the software program that Dominic had created to debug any system, companies feared that his company was weak without him at the helm. His presence proved critical to his company's growth and maintenance. Every day his company lost millions because of his being held in jail without bail.

Trying to help her friend, Jamila introduced Donna to a friend of hers. His name was Richard Smith, a divorce attorney. Jamila never tried to convince Donna she should leave Dominic, but she wanted her to have the support if needed. That's why she introduced them.

But Donna was reluctant to talk to him. She still had hope that Dominic was innocent and that they could rebuild their family. She wanted her life back for Dawson's sake, but a part of her was ready to move on.

"Hello, Mrs. Jones." Richard extended his hand. "Jamila has told me a lot about you."

Donna shook his hand and felt the wind knocked out of her. The minute she met Richard she was attracted to him.

"It's nice to meet you as well." *He's so handsome, intelligent, and a gentleman. Why now?*

"I'll let you two talk." Jamila excused herself from The Jones's patio. *Read the signs, girl.*

"You have such a beautiful home. I know this is kind of awkward meeting me now, but when you get ready I'll be waiting."

"Excuse me?" *He can't read my mind, can he?*

"About your divorce."

"Oh that." Even though Donna wasn't ready to accept her marriage was over, she didn't see the harm in talking to Richard.

"It can be rough. Trust me, I know. Here's my card. Call me some time." Richard couldn't deny he was attracted to Donna. She was so beautiful, her long black hair reminding him of a Native American princess.

There definitely was some tension in the air, but Donna tried to fight it. She fanned herself with her hand. "It feels hot out here. Maybe we should go inside."

"I know what you mean. Listen, I won't take up too much of your time. Like I said, when you're ready to talk, call me." *I hope you do.*

Donna agreed to meet Richard at his office in Roxbury the following week. She was impressed that his office was located in the heart of Boston and that he didn't conform to the silly notion that a successful lawyer had to work at one of the big-time firms downtown.

His waiting area was comfortable with a black leather sofa and loveseat. He had a coffee table full of *Ebony, Essence, Vibe, US Weekly* and *People* magazines. He also had a large fish tank with exotic fish swimming around aimlessly. Every time someone got up to get a cup of water, the gallons of water in the tank would make a soft droning noise that flowed with the sounds of Earth, Wind & Fire playing an instrumental in the background. Pictures of the million-man march, Dr. Martin Luther King, Malcolm X, Nelson Mandela, and Oprah Winfrey hung on the walls.

Donna felt a growing admiration for a man she barely new. Something about his style and the way he shook her hand with his smile made her feel warm inside.

"Mr. Smith is ready to see you now, Mrs. Jones," Richard's secretary told her.

Donna didn't know what came over her, but she felt the need to run to the bathroom real quick to check her makeup and clothes. She was excited to see him. "I need to use the restroom."

"It's down the hall to your left."

When Donna quickly ran to the bathroom, the secretary then told Richard, "Mrs. Jones will be right in, in a few moments."

After Donna finished primping, she glanced into the mirror one last time. "Get it together." She patted her hair and pulled down her skirt and fixed her blouse one last time for real. She walked into Richard's office, nervous as hell. *What the heck is the matter with you?* Donna had feelings she hadn't felt before in a very long time.

Richard stood up, shook her hand and gave her that same warm, friendly smile. He closed his office door. "Have a seat. I'm glad you decided to meet with me after all. I know divorce can be tough, but I'm here to make it easier for you."

Donna was in la-la land, busy checking Richard out, acting like a lovesick schoolgirl, but once she heard the word *divorce*, she snapped out of it. "Who said anything about divorce? I'm not ready to make that decision."

Richard understood Donna's uncertainty, because he had gone through a heart-breaking divorce as well. "I understand, Donna. Do you want to talk about your marriage?"

"To you? I don't know. I think I should leave that to my psychologist."

"It's been that hard for you, hasn't it? I sought professional help after my divorce, too. It was the hardest thing I had to go through. It still pains me sometimes."

"How long were you married?"

"About seventeen years. She was my high-school sweetheart. We married when we were eighteen, had a baby when we were nineteen. I went to college and law school, and she stayed at home with the baby. Before I knew it, she started to resent me for my success and felt like our marriage was suffocating her. She wanted to explore other options out there for her, so after our son went off to college, she filed for divorce."

"That must have been very hard."

"I was devastated. I should have seen it coming. I was too busy climbing the corporate ladder, trying to make partner, working fifty hours a week, barely spending time with my family. Now I've got my own firm and all the time in the world, but it's too late."

"Do you ever think things are the way they are for a reason? Like life paths that are laid before your feet?"

"I know what you mean. Either you take them, or you run from them."

"I think I've been running from mine all my life."

"How so?"

Donna told Richard everything about her marriage, from how she and Dominic met, to the hysterectomy, battling depression, her deferred dreams, and how she stood by and let Dominic do whatever he wanted. She told him things about her marriage that she'd never even admitted to herself.

Feeling instantly connected to him, they talked for hours. He became a friend, her compadre, and for the first time in a very long time, Donna really smiled. She saw the sign.

Later that week, Donna visited Dominic in jail to give him updates about Dawson. Their entire visit would be about him trying to make her feel sad for him that he was in jail, and reassuring her that life would be different. Every time she asked him to admit his affair with Tera, he continued to deny it, saying he was framed.

Donna was tired of Dominic's lies and wanted her life as Mrs. Jones to be over, but she felt a duty to stick by her husband, even though she knew he was the most self-centered bastard on the planet.

"So are you telling me you didn't get that woman pregnant?" Donna asked for the umpteenth time.

"Baby, you know I can't discuss the case, but no, for the last time, I wasn't seeing her."

"So why did you refuse to have your blood taken?"

"How did you know about that?"

"Luke's not only *your* attorney, you know. I ask him about what's going on and he tells me. I need to know, you know."

"No, I don't know. You need to stand by your husband and not let silly rumors enter your head. You know how much I love you."

"Save it, Dominic. You only love yourself. And if you didn't father her child, then you *would* take the blood test."

Donna was growing more and more disgusted by the second. She contemplated divorce and wanted to explore a relationship with Richard, but her values wouldn't allow her to actually go through with it.

"You believe me, don't you? You know I didn't do anything to that woman."

"I don't know what I believe."

"What about you? You had just as much motive as I did." Desperate, Dominic was ready to sell out his own mother, if she were alive, to get out of his predicament.

Donna got up from the table and summoned the guard. "Dominic, you can rot in hell."

"Baby, wait, I didn't mean it. I'm sorry. Wait."

"What is it?"

"I have these pictures in my office. I need you to take good care of them."

Donna knew exactly what pictures he was referring to and couldn't believe what he wanted her to do. "Fuck you, Dominic. They found those a long time ago, so your dirty little secret is out."

"Then you know they are fake. You saw them, right? You saw what she was trying to do."

"What I saw was who I really married. And now I have to decide what to do about it."

"What do you mean?"

"Goodbye, Dominic."

"Wait, Donna."

Donna left the jail and Dominic behind. She was beginning to feel the weight come off, but knew, as with any program, it was going to take some time to see the results. She just hoped everything fit when all the weight was completely off. If not, she would just have to go shopping for new things in her life.

Chapter 32

Weeks before Dominic's trial, Donna started noticing that Dawson was getting worse. Her grades were slipping (she scored a mere 750 on her PSAT), and she quit the cheerleading squad. Donna knew this was a rough time for her daughter but didn't want her to miss out on the opportunity to get into a good college and move on with her life. She tried not to nag her too much, but she couldn't let her daughter end up like her. She pushed Dawson and pushed, but Dawson always ran out on their conversation, refusing to listen. She always cried at the mention of her father and refused to go see him in jail, and would get very angry whenever she read anything about him or Tera in the newspaper.

The following week Donna got a call from Dawson's school. She'd been suspended for fighting. When Dawson got home, Donna almost lost her mind. She'd had enough of Dawson's acting out and was tired of tiptoeing around her because of her father.

"Dawson Dominique Jones, we need to have a major talk."

"I'm not in the mood for one of your lectures, Donna." Dawson walked past her mother and went into the kitchen.

Donna's temperature rose. All the suppressed anger about Dominic's infidelity, his lies, his betrayal poured out of her and landed on the first person within reach.

Dawson was drinking a glass of water when Donna entered the kitchen. She rolled her eyes at her mother.

Donna snatched the glass of water out of her hand and threw it into her daughter's face. Then she smacked her.

Dawson held her face in shock.

"Now you listen to me, you little brat. I've had enough of you. I know it's hard for you, but it's hard for me, too. We are going to get through this together. We are all we've got. If you think I'm going to let you disrespect me, then you've really lost your mind."

Dawson got up and headed toward the door.

Donna pulled her back by her shirt. "Sit your little ass down. When I'm finished with you, then you can leave."

Dawson wiggled and tried to struggle. "Leave me alone," she said, but Donna overpowered her.

"Stop your whining. So what? Someone at your school said something about your father? Is that why you fought? I know it is."

"Yeah. So what?"

"So what? Dawson, just because everyone is acting like an asshole doesn't mean you have to. What did the girl say?"

"It doesn't matter. She's wrong anyway. They're all wrong." Dawson had an evil grin on her face.

"Dawson, I'm going to visit your father tomorrow. You should go with me. I think it will help you, if you could—"

Dawson's grin was replaced by a frown. "I'm not going. I don't want to see him. I can't."

"Why not?"

"Because I can't. I can't."

"Honey, I know it's hard, but you have to face your demons. You won't be able to get on with your life, unless you—"

"I can't," Dawson said, crying.

"Honey, you have to. Your father needs you."

"I can't. I hate him. I hate her. She deserved it."

"Don't say that."

"Admit it, Mom, you wanted her gone just as much as any of us did. You just didn't have the guts to do something about it."

"Dawson, I'm one heartbeat from smacking the shit out of you again. Don't talk to me like that. How dare you?"

"She was going to destroy our family. She deserved it, Mommy." Dawson began to cry harder.

Donna hugged her. "It's going to be okay, baby, let it out. It's going to be okay."

"No, it's not. You don't understand. Daddy's going to jail forever, and it's all my fault."

"What are you talking about?"

Hysterical, Dawson broke away, her face wet with tears. She started to pull her hair out.

"Dawson, honey, stop it. Sit down. It's going to be okay."

"No, it's not. It's all my fault."

"No, it isn't. You didn't make your father have an affair. You can't blame yourself."

"But he didn't do it."

"I know, honey. He'll be fine."

"No, he won't." Dawson began to shake her head, and

191

globs of snot ran out of her nose. "She said Daddy was never going to get out and that he would be gang-raped like a little bitch." Dawson cried harder as she fell to the floor.

"Who said that? The girl at your school?"

Dawson nodded. "It's all my fault."

Donna bent to the floor and grabbed her weeping daughter in a tight hug. "It's not your fault. You mustn't blame yourself for what your father did." She felt her daughter's pain and wished she could remove it, but she couldn't.

"He didn't do it."

"I know, sweetie. Hush now. "

"No, Mommy, he didn't do it. I did."

Donna was still. A chill ran through her body, and her heart felt like it was cut in her throat. "What are you talking about?"

Dawson couldn't stop crying, she was more hysterical than before. It was like the memory was too painful to put into words. She tried to stop crying so she could speak. Her moaning muffled her words. "I killed Daddy's girlfriend."

"What?"

"When Daddy left, I hid in his car. I knew he was going to see her. I didn't want her to take him away from us."

Dawson was sobbing so much that Donna could barely understand her. "What are you saying?"

"I heard them arguing, and then Daddy started to beat on her with a bottle. I saw him." She cried harder and harder. "I waited until Daddy left her, then I went in. She cursed at me and told me that Daddy didn't love us and he would soon be with her and their baby. We fought and fought and then"—Dawson started to tremble.

"And then what?"

"I blacked out and when I woke up she was dead." Dawson let out a loud wail.

Donna couldn't believe what she said. "It's okay, honey. You didn't hurt anyone it was all a dream."

"No, it wasn't. I shot her."

"What? How?"

"When I woke up I had a gun in my hand and she was dead."

"No, sweetie, it was a dream. It had to be."

"No, it wasn't," Dawson shouted. Then she broke away from her mother and ran.

Donna ran after her and followed her to her bedroom. "Dawson, wait."

Dawson rifled through her book bag, and when she turned around with a .38 caliber in her trembling hand. "Do you believe me now?"

"Where did you get that?" Donna asked, terrified. "Give it to me."

"I hid it at school so the police wouldn't find it when they searched the house. I killed her and now Daddy is going to jail forever. It's my entire fault. I hated her, I hate myself." Dawson kept sobbing.

"Honey, give me the gun."

Dawson held it to her head. "I can't take this anymore. I wish I was dead, too."

"Dawson, don't. Honey, stop. I love you. It's going to be fine." Donna moved slowly toward her.

She shook her head still crying. "I don't. I can't."

Donna rushed her. "Baby, stop."

BANG!

Chapter 33

Donna finally took Richard up on his offer and gave him a call. He was pleased to hear from her, both professionally and personally, and agreed to meet with her for dinner to discuss her pressing matter.

Legal Sea Foods wasn't crowded this Monday evening. It was rainy and the chill of winter was settling in. Donna could hardly finish her mussels as she broke out in tears.

"You will get through this, Donna," Richard told her. "I'm here for you. Don't worry, I'm going to take care of everything."

Donna dried her eyes. She was so happy she'd met Richard.

"You know what you have to do now?" Richard asked.

Donna sighed. "I have to have a talk with my husband," she said reluctantly.

The next day at the South Boston jail, Donna patiently waited to have a meeting with her husband. Richard came with her as her attorney to set up a meeting with Dominic in private.

Once Dominic entered the small brick-walled room, the prison officer left and locked the door. Dominic looked surprised. He thought he was meeting with his lawyer. Disappointed, he said, "Hello."

Richard handed him his business card. "Hello, Mr. Jones. I'm Richard Smith, your wife's attorney."

"You want a divorce?" Dominic held back his tears as he looked at Donna, his heart tightening inside his chest.

"Could you leave us alone for a minute, Richard?"

Richard obliged and signaled for the guard to open the door.

Once alone with his wife, Dominic tried to plead his case. "Donna, I'm fighting for my life. I can't stand losing you right now."

"I know, Dominic, but—"

"But what? You can just throw away fifteen years?"

"Listen, things have changed. I found out—"

"Baby, I'm innocent. I may have fooled around on you carelessly, but I didn't murder her. You have to believe me." *I thought I did, but the cunt was still breathing apparently.*

"I do believe you. I always have." Donna whispered in his ear. "I know who did."

Dominic almost fell out of his chair. "You do?"

"But it doesn't matter because I'll never turn her in."

"Woman, don't make me choke it out of you."

Maybe a few months ago when Donna couldn't stand herself, let alone respect herself, she would have given in to her husband's threat. Maybe if she were still the woman who looked the other way when her husband openly cheated on her, she would have given him anything he wanted. Maybe if she still lived to please him and felt guilty about losing her womb, she would have compromised. But not today. Her Prozac was at a therapeutic level, and she was now motivated to protect the one person who mattered to her more than life itself.

"Dominic, what I'm about to tell you is going to shock you. I still can't believe it myself, but it's the truth."

Dominic's heart was racing, and his stomach was turning. "What?"

"You know how that night we thought Dawson was sleeping in her room after our fight?"

"Yeah."

"Well, she wasn't in her room. She hid in your back seat and followed you to that woman's apartment. She waited and watched you beat her, until her own anger drove her mad."

"Baby, no."

"Yes. She shot her. You drove your only daughter to murder. She did what we both couldn't do."

Dominic began to cry. "I can't believe this. This can't be happening."

"I thought she was lying or dreaming. But she knew things about the murder that were never discussed on the news. She had the gun, Dominic, all this time."

"What are we going to do?"

"Dawson is going to get psychiatric help, and you are going to have to take the fall for her. Leave our daughter out of it."

"Are you crazy? They will sentence me to death."

"They won't if you plead guilty to a lesser charge."

"I'm not pleading anything."

"Oh yes, the hell you are. I've sacrificed, Dawson's sacrificed, and now it's your turn."

"But I'm innocent."

"Of murder, yes, but not of all your other unspeakable crimes. For those you are guilty."

"But she wouldn't get any time, she's a minor."

"I'm not about to place my child's life in the hands of the law. You don't know how things could go. They could try her as an adult and then what would happen to her? I'm not sending my only child to death row."

"But you would send me? Honey, trust me, she won't get any time, she would be fine."

"She tried to kill herself, Dominic."

"What?"

"When she told me, she put a gun to her head and pulled the trigger. I saved her just in time. She was sickened with guilt for you being in here and she being the one to have done what she did. Our daughter is not well. She will not make it through a trial. She inherited my unstable mood and your ego. The two are a deadly combination. She is going to therapy to deal with this. People will think she needs it because her father is in jail." Donna folded her arms and shook her head. "Plead to manslaughter and you'll be out in a few years."

"And what about my company? What about us? How will you survive if I'm in prison?"

"That's why I brought Richard. When this is all over, I'm filing for divorce. I figure if they see your family is still supporting you, they will go easier on you. After you are sentenced, I'm selling your company and taking my share. I will put the rest in a interest-bearing account, so when you do get out, you will be able to start over."

"I see you have it all figured out. You forgot one thing, though—I'm Dominic Jones and I'm not going to stand by and watch you destroy me."

Donna laughed. "You destroyed yourself, Dominic. You have no one to blame but yourself. It's because of you our daughter tried to commit suicide, it's because of you that she did what she did, and it's because of you that woman is dead."

"I won't let you do this to me. There has to be another way. I'm so sorry for what happened to Dawson, but I know I can fix it. I won't let you do this."

"Watch me. I've been your doormat for too long. I've tried to love you and make you a better person, but you're not worth it. Finally I see you for who you are, Dominic, and even now, you're still trying to cut corners, willing to risk our only child going to prison."

"I love Dawson more than you know. It's not my fault you can't have any more children."

Donna slapped him. "You are nothing but a spiteful bastard and you deserve everything that's coming to you. You've cheated on me for years and knocked up and aborted God knows how many babies and you can lecture me on my reproductive capabilities? Fuck you, Dominic." Donna began to cry, hurting from all the years she'd allowed him to disrespect her, all the years she'd wasted trying to love him and keep their family together.

"I'm sorry, Donna, really, but I need you now. I need Dawson. Let's stay together. I can fix this."

"No, you can't. It's too late."

"Baby, please . . . I'm begging you."

"I won't stand by and let you destroy our daughter too. For years I chose you, Dominic, because I thought it was love. And now I see it wasn't. Finally, I'm awake and alive again, and it's either you or Dawson. I choose her. I choose love."

"You won't make it without me. You won't survive. You can't leave me."

Donna dried her eyes. "Oh shut up, Dominic. For once in your life, do the right thing. Don't fight me on this. Plead guilty to a lesser charge and you will live to see another day." Donna signaled for the guard.

Dominic was devastated.

She turned and looked at him one last time. "Goodbye, Dominic," she said and headed for the door, finally free.

Dominic looked at his wife in defeat. He stared at the door she'd walked through for as long as he could. Then the guard collected him and brought him back to his lonely cell. He felt the lump in his throat, and tears streamed down his face. He was sad for himself and for his only daughter. But he was mostly sad for taking his family and his life for granted. He'd been careless with the women in his life. He'd felt that he disappointed his father and let down the one person who'd loved him unconditionally, Dawson.

The next day he called Luke and told him he wanted to plead guilty to manslaughter.

Epilogue

Dominic was sentenced to eight years in prison. He used his time wisely by teaching computer classes to inmates. He wrote at least once a week to Dawson, telling her how much he loved her and not to worry about him. He told her she shouldn't feel bad about what happened, that it was all his fault, and that he deserved to be where he is. He encouraged her to go to college and make him proud. He also warned her about not latching on to a man, and to be her own woman. Strong enough never to marry a man like her father.

After divorcing Dominic, Donna dated Richard for a year. When he proposed, Donna was happier than ever. She and Richard moved to Atlanta to get away from all the bad memories of Boston. With her settlement money, she opened a dance school in Buckhead and taught students ages five through twenty-one, finally accomplishing her goal, feeling more independent now, even though she remarried. Richard treated Donna as his equal, and Donna couldn't think of any other way a marriage should work.

Dawson completed psychological treatment after two years and got into Princeton. Although she still couldn't bring herself to visit her father in prison, she wrote him and sent him pictures of herself. She majored in psychology, focusing on child and family psychology. Her Prozac kept her mood stable and she tried to move on with her life. She even had a boyfriend. She heeded her parents' advice and put school first before boys.

She understood why her father took the fall for her, but still felt guilty. She even confessed to her psychologist, who wouldn't believe her. Dawson's mind was still fuzzy from that night. Her doctor attributed her flights of fantasy to the stress of her father in prison and other adolescent problems. Although she still had nightmares now and then, she was coping with the fact that she murdered her father's girl-friend and her parents covered it up. Dawson fought depression every day and tried to keep the Jones family secret, wondering how long she could live like this.

After Dominic was convicted, Mark asked Shaniece out on a date.

He wanted Dominic to get life, but was satisfied that he would serve time and not get away with murder. He let go of some of his anger and was able to find love again in Shaniece. He planned on asking her to marry him as soon as the time was right.

Shaniece visited her cousin's grave every year on her birthday and brought her yellow roses, Tera's favorite. One time, Shaniece sat for hours talking to her cousin's tombstone as she drank a bottle of wine. "Isn't it funny how things turned out, Tera?" she said. "After all your bragging and boasting about being a girlfriend and how it is better, you get killed over it. I bet you didn't see that coming. I bet in your wildest dreams you didn't think you'd finally get what you deserved. It was too easy, though, knocking that little girl out, shooting you, and then putting the gun in her hand. I thought for sure she'd cave, but lo and behold, her father took the blame. Nonetheless, I got away with it. It must suck to know that I killed you and your precious Dominic is behind bars. But hey, what goes around comes around, bitch. You should have never fucked with me and maybe you wouldn't be dead. But you are, and I've met the most wonderful man because of it. So, thank you, cousin. Thank you for bringing Mark and me together. He loves me so much, and I'm sure he's going to propose sooner or later. And when he finally makes me his wife, I'll be so glad that a conniving, low-down whore like you isn't around to be his girlfriend."